THE HUNTSMAN

Douglas Hill was born and raised in a small city in western Canada. After graduating in English, he moved in 1959 to London, where he still lives, and worked in publishing before becoming a full-time writer. He became addicted to science fiction at an early age – by reading comics like Flash Gordon – and has remained a hopeless addict ever since. In the early sixties he began reviewing science fiction regularly for *Tribune* at a time when the national press barely acknowledged the existence of SF.

He was literary editor of *Tribune* for several years, and is the renowned author of more than fifty books for adults and children.

DOUGLAS HILL

WARRIORS OF THE WASTELAND

THE HUNTSMAN

**MACMILLAN
CHILDREN'S BOOKS**

First published 1982 by William Heinemann Ltd

Published 1984 by Pan
This edition published 1997 by Macmillan Children's Books
a division of Macmillan Publishers Ltd
25 Eccleston Place, London SW1W 9NF
and Basingstoke

Associated companies throughout the world

ISBN 0 330 35384 5

1 3 5 7 9 8 6 4 2

A CIP catalogue record for this book is available from
the British Library.

Printed by Mackays of Chatham plc, Kent

For Jill Mackay,
who made things happen

Prologue

IT HAD BEEN a pleasant day for Joshua Ferral. The sun had risen warm to take the chill out of the October air, yet left it crisp, fresh and fragrant. Most of the trees in the dense forest were wearing their most fanciful autumn colours, and it had seemed that all of the riches of the wilds, as well as the beauties, had been there for the taking. Josh's big leather knapsack was bulging with fresh meat – and there were some special portions that he had marked out for himself, for his wife Myra to work her cookery magic on.

He was a man of middle height and middle age, lean and brown, with a streak or two of grey in his thick dark hair. He wore a plain shirt and trousers of deerskin, and low boots made from some more sturdy leather. A keen-bladed knife was belted at his hip, and in one hand he carried a long, slender pole, with a sharpened and fire-hardened point that identified it as a spear. And he moved through the forest with an easy, smooth stride, almost noiselessly despite the carpeting of fallen leaves, seeming perfectly at home.

As he did so often, Josh felt grateful – not to any one in particular, just grateful. That the wilderness gave of its bounty so generously. That he had the skills that were needed to live off that bounty. Of course, it meant a busy and often hard life for him, since the entire village depended on his skills for the fresh meat that they needed to fill out their diet. And, in a way, that set him apart from the rest of the villagers.

But that rarely troubled Josh. They were small-minded, often mean-minded folk, stuck into the patches of dirt that they scraped at to help feed themselves, not knowing or caring what lay beyond the edge of their village – too scared of their own shadows ever to want to know.

Well, maybe not, Josh thought, to be fair. It wasn't *their* shadows that they feared, but the shadow that lay over the whole world, the shadow all mankind feared. Or what was left of mankind.

But it was no time to think about fear and shadows, on a beautiful October day when the hunting had been so good. It was a big country – Josh knew more than most people how big it was, for he had wandered a bit as a young man, even though it was considered a risky thing to do. He had seen for himself how far the wilderness stretched – wilderness that was only occasionally interrupted by one of the small, huddled villages which were all that remained of man's presence. A man could live his life in peace – safe from shadows, from fear – in that wilderness. Unless his luck turned bad, or he did something careless or stupid.

And while Josh Ferral had taken a few risks in his time, he was never careless or stupid.

At the moment, for instance, though he seemed to be ambling idly through the trees and the lush undergrowth, Josh's eyes never stopped moving. Not a leaf stirred, not a twig shifted, but those sharp eyes looked, examined, carefully assessed. There was always the chance of meeting a bear, wildcat, even a rare wolverine. But Josh knew that most times even those animals will leave men alone, if men leave them alone. And Josh was normally willing to go out of his way to do just that.

So when he skirted a tangle of fallen logs and briars, and saw the bush, with its ripe burden of bright red berries, being shaken violently by something unseen, he stopped in his tracks.

Not a bear, he thought to himself, after a silent moment of careful study. Too small, down too low. Maybe a raccoon. Maybe it won't mind if I take some berries back to Myra.

He moved forward, soundlessly, poising the crude spear just in case. With its point, he gently parted the branches of the bush. And both his mouth and his eyes opened wide with astonishment.

It was not a bear, not a raccoon. It was a baby boy.

Somewhere between two and three years old, Josh reckoned. Chubby, healthy, and bare as the day he was born. Dirt-stained, berry-stained, and not in the least troubled by the fact that he was all alone in the middle of the wilderness.

The child saw Josh, and stopped its greedy snatching at the berries to stare with round, curious grey eyes that showed not a scrap of fear. Josh moved closer, kneeling down to look into the small, berry-smeared face.

"Now, by all that's livin'," he whispered, half to himself, "where'd *you* come from, young fella?"

At the sound of his voice, the baby smiled, and held out a small fist, filled with mashed and dripping berries.

"That's mighty nice of y'," Josh said, smiling in return. "Y' seem to be lookin' after y'rself real good, for a little 'un."

He glanced round. In a narrow gap within the berry bushes there was a pile of dry leaves, which Josh could see had not come there naturally. And a fragment or two of leaf caught in the child's tangled thatch of straw-coloured hair showed that the leaves had served as a bed. Josh shook his head, mystified. Though the boy had clearly spent a chilly autumn night stark naked, with nothing but leaves to keep him warm, he showed no ill effects. But had he gathered the leaves for himself? Had he been naked when he got there? And just how *did* he get there?

Watched intently by the child, Josh made a quick scrutiny of the ground around the berry bush. His skill showed him a sign or two where a small bare foot had left a trace. But there were no other signs. If the ground wasn't hiding some secret from him, it looked like the boy had just come toddling along, till he found himself a place to nest.

A thought struck Josh, like ice sliding down his spine. He glanced up at the clear sky. Could the boy have been *dropped* into the forest, by *Them*?

But the thought made no sense. *They* didn't put humans into the forest – *they* took humans out. And yet the boy's presence also made no sense. But he was there – and Josh was not going to walk away and leave him.

He held out a hand to the child. "C'mon then, little mystery man," he said with a smile. "You'n me better get on home – an' see if Myra c'n find some clothes for y'."

For a moment the child gazed up at him, the clear grey eyes grave, as if weighing him up. Then he grinned and chuckled, and held up both arms to be picked up.

Josh laughed, and swung him up, settling him against his hip. As he did so, he noticed the odd mark on the boy's left arm, up near the shoulder. A group of small, dark dots, standing out clearly against the fair skin – and seeming to be arranged in some kind of pattern. But the pattern meant nothing to Josh.

He rubbed a thumb thoughtfully over the dots, and again, for no reason at all, he felt a chill along his spine. But the boy chuckled, untroubled, bouncing up and down as if eager to be on their way.

So Josh turned and strode off through the forest towards home. This'll make a few people nervous in the village, he thought wryly. But I reckon Myra'll take one look at him an' make up her mind t' keep him. An' then we'll have to start worryin' that his real folks might come along lookin' for him.

But he knew that was not too likely. His village hadn't been visited by a stranger in years. And the nearest village to his was more than fifty kilometres away – much farther than most people those days would dare to travel.

"So I reckon, young fella," he said aloud, "y' got y'rself a new home an' new folks. An' y'll be welcome. Me an' Myra, we been hopin' t' have kids, but we ain't been lucky so far. I reckon now we got us one – even if it's a sorta peculiar way t' do it."

He smiled down at the boy in his arms, who was gazing with bright-eyed fascination at the forest around them.

"An' I'll bet y' anythin' y' like," Josh continued, as he strode on, "that Myra'll want t' name y' after her old pa. Finn. That suit y'? Finn Ferral . . ."

1

The Taking

A STRAY FEATHER of wind rattled the topmost leaves of poplars, adding its sound to the birdsong and insect hum among the shadowed branches – the sounds of the forest's perpetual murmuring to itself, as it drowsed in the mid-morning sun of an early summer day. From the crest of a tall pine, a hawk rose to make a splash of red and brown against the sky's unblemished blue, before arrowing away westward – where the wilderness marched on to the horizon, farther even than the hawk's keen eye could see. And below, on the sun-dappled edge of a glade, a small deer with new antlers still half-velvet stood warily still, nose lifted, ears swivelling.

Downwind from the glade, a young man moved through the leafy dimness among the trees – moved at an easy, un-hurried pace, but in complete and uncanny silence, so that not even the nervous deer was aware of his presence. Yet he had noticed the deer, just as he had glimpsed the hawk, just as he was able to single out, and identify, each one of the mingled sounds of the forest.

The young man was compactly muscled, lean and lithe as a healthy wolf, with a thatch of straw-coloured hair and grey eyes beneath strong brows. He wore a simple deerskin jerkin and leggings, and low soft boots; at one hip hung a heavy knife, at the other, a deerskin pouch.

And around his left wrist was wrapped a broad strip of darker, sturdier leather.

He was not yet twenty years old, yet by profession he was the huntsman for his village, which lay about two kilometres away to the east. But he was not hunting today. He had been briefly tempted at the sight of the deer, so that his right hand had strayed to the rawhide wrapping on his other wrist, revealing it to be a crude but serviceable sling. But in the end he had rewrapped the sling, and left the deer alone. Game had been plentiful lately, and the village larders were groaning with fresh meat, so that many of the villagers were fully occupied salting portions of the meat, storing it for winter, or drying and curing the hides.

So the young man was able to come into the forest to indulge in his favourite pastime – wandering, drifting, idly turning the pages of the endless and ever-changing book of the wilderness. His name was Finn Ferral – and he had been studying that book all of his young life.

Before he had left the village, his father, Joshua Ferral – in fact his foster father, though Finn seldom thought of him that way – had asked him to look for a straight sapling of ash or maple that would make a new handle for a hoe. And at first he had also had it in mind to look in some of the hollows for early violets, which he knew would brighten the blue eyes of Josh's daughter, Jena, six years Finn's junior.

But in the depths of the forest, he had forgotten about hoe-handles and flowers. Despite the tranquillity that surrounded him, despite the fact that he knew this part of the wilderness as intimately as he knew the main room of his home, he felt uneasy.

Something was different about the forest. There was a wrongness – an ominous feeling, as if the leafy shadows held some hidden menace. He wondered if the young deer felt it, too, for it had seemed unusually tense and watchful. Perhaps even the hawk had felt it, before it had sped away. Yet so far he had seen or heard nothing out of the ordinary, which might explain the feeling; and had detected no unusual scents on the light breeze.

But forest creatures seem to rely on more than just their five senses. And Finn Ferral was as much a forest creature as he was a man.

He moved towards a steep slope that would lead him to higher and more open ground, to give him a broader view of the forest expanses. As he climbed, drifting through the undergrowth as always in total silence and near-invisibility, he swivelled constantly to study every bit of foliage and ground around him, his usual watchful alertness raised even higher by the continuing feeling of unease. Soon he came up to a patch of open sunlit turf near the top of the ridge, and there he glimpsed tendrils of grey smoke, rising lazily in the distance from the chimneys of his village.

Then he caught sight of something else, which froze him where he stood, lifting and bristling the hairs on the back of his neck.

Two bat-winged shapes, swooping and circling among the drifting strands of smoke.

They were tiny in the distance, but Finn's eyes, no less keen than the hawk's, could make them out. He had seen such shapes only twice before in his life, always far away. But he knew what they were.

Swiftly he sprang up the rest of the slope to the ridge top. And again he froze still, while the breath caught in his suddenly constricted throat.

Now he could see all of the village, seeming doll-sized at that distance – a cluster of small dwellings within a broad, dusty clearing. Near its centre was the wooden surround and cover of the communal well. And near the well lay something that Finn knew, beyond question, was the source of his feeling of ominous menace.

An egg-shaped, metallic object, seeming big enough to fit four people into, glittering balefully in the sun.

It was something that Finn had never seen before. Yet he also knew what it was, and what its presence meant.

They had come to the village.

Finn was hardly aware of launching himself into a headlong dash down the slope. Nor did he have any idea of why he was running, or what he intended to do. But he ran with all of his surefooted speed, weaving like a brown blur among the treetrunks.

Even so, many minutes passed before he had covered the distance back to the village. As he reached the little cluster of houses, he saw that the metal object was no longer there, the bat-winged creatures no longer in sight. And nothing seemed to be changed. The houses – mostly cabins made from peeled logs, with low thatched roofs – stood as solidly as ever, and smoke still rose quietly from their chimneys.

But the doors of many of the cabins stood ajar, and there was a knot of people on the far side of the village. And Finn could hear the sound of weeping.

His eyes went at once to the cabin nearest to him, on the edge of the village – his home, for as long as he could remember. Its door, too, was open, but there was no sign of movement within, no glimpse of Josh's grizzled head, no sound of Jena's bright voice.

They would be among the crowd of village folk, he told himself. He did not let himself think where else they might be.

The crowd turned towards Finn as he drew near. Most of the faces were drawn and fearful, and he saw tears in the eyes of many, men and women. And in other eyes he saw expressions of bitterness and rage.

"What's happened here?" Finn called.

A burly, bearded man stepped forward, his mouth twisted in a snarl. "Death's been here, is what. And the fault of it be down to *you*, Finn Ferral!"

As Finn blinked with shock and puzzlement, a tall man in the crowd held up a hand. "That's crazy, Hocker. Weren't no fault of the boy's." He turned to Finn. "An evil day, lad. Slavers 've been."

"An' burned my Bethie!" roared the bearded man called Hocker.

Only then did Finn see the crumpled form of the woman, lying in the dust half-hidden by the throng of villagers. The sight squeezed his throat like a clamp.

"Why?" he whispered. "Why did they?"

"'Cause you wasn't here, Finn Ferral, is why!" roared Hocker.

Again the tall man intervened. "Slavers took young Lyle," he said gruffly. "Bethie tried to stop 'em, him bein' her only son an' all. They burned her."

Shaken, Finn looked at Hocker. "I'm sorry . . ."

"You'll know sorrow enough," Hocker shouted. "You'll not live without a care while my boy's taken and my Bethie's burned!" Tears spilled from the big man's eyes, but there was as much fury as grief blazing from them.

Wordless, astonished, Finn turned to the tall man, who shrugged and sighed.

"Ain't your fault, Finn." The crowd murmured, whether in agreement or otherwise Finn could not be sure. "Hocker just figgers if you'd been here, Slavers would've taken you 'stead of Lyle."

Finn stared without understanding.

The tall man gazed back bleakly. "Then y' don't know yet?"

"Know what?" Finn asked. But even before the tall man began to explain, the realization struck him like a blow from an axe.

"Thing is, lad, Slavers must've come for three, 'cause they took three. An' it might've been you 'stead of Lyle — 'cause first two they took was old Josh and Jena."

2

A World Enslaved

FINN SWAYED, AND his vision blurred. Hocker was bellowing again, and other villagers were speaking all at once, but their voices were only a distant roaring in his ears. His body was numb, icy with shock. Half-blinded by sudden tears, he turned and stumbled away.

Behind him Hocker roared, "There's a blood debt owed for this day, Finn Ferral!"

And then he was lunging after Finn, a knife appearing in his hand.

Even in the depths of anguish and horror, some instinct warned Finn. He turned, meeting Hocker's rush – and though he was flung back by the big man's weight, one hand flashed out to clamp on the meaty wrist of Hocker's knife hand. Then Finn planted his feet, and Hocker found himself stopped in his tracks, gasping in pain as the steely grip on his wrist tightened and twisted. The knife fell, glinting in the dust.

"Where was your killing, Hocker, when Slavers were here?" Finn's voice was harsh, unrecognizable. "What of the blood debt *they* owe?"

Without apparent effort, he flung the burly man away, sending him sprawling wide-eyed on the ground. Then Finn looked at the others, and saw the truth in their faces. Some were sullen, some afraid, some merely watchful. But nearly all, he saw, were ranged against him. They had to hate something, after the day's terror. And he was the scapegoat – because he was the outsider, no kin to any of them, no real part of their narrow, fearful lives.

He turned and strode away, towards the cabin that had been his home. When he had closed the door, he let himself sag back against it, while the emptiness of the place closed in around him, cold and desolate. The emptiness – and the memories . . .

Always before, the cabin had been full – of love and warmth, caring and belonging. Ever since the day when Joshua Ferral had brought him home from the forest. Finn remembered nothing of what had happened to him before that day. But he remembered how Myra had wrapped him in the warmth of her welcome, and how she and Josh had taken him as their own. Over the years that followed they had raised him with love, and had taken unending pleasure from his lively cheerfulness, and from his quick, curious mind that always seemed hungry to learn everything about everything.

Most especially, in those growing years, Finn had wanted to learn from Josh about the ways of the wilderness. And he learned so swiftly that Josh had come to believe that the child had a special, almost mystical link with the wilds – perhaps growing out of that time when he had wandered alone in the forest and miraculously survived its dangers.

As the years had passed, and the boy grew tall and strong, it was only natural that he should become Josh Ferral's successor as the village huntsman. And it also became necessary, when Myra fell ill after giving birth to her daughter, Jena. It was an illness that might once have been swept aside with a few pills, but there were no such cures in the world where Myra lived. Within a year she was dead. And then Josh, older now and slower, and with a baby to tend, was ready to stay at home and leave the hunting to the skills of young Finn.

"I taught that boy, but now he can teach me," Josh would say to his neighbours. "He can count the feathers on a hawk so high maybe we couldn't see it. He can hear a mouse breathin' underground, track a beaver through water. Never saw the like."

The neighbours would nod and smile, but glance at each other – not because Josh was boasting, for they knew he spoke the simple truth, but because there was something about Finn Ferral that unsettled them.

And old Josh would smile to himself and say, "He's a grand lad, and I like t' have him around, but when he's home I kinda feel sorry. It's like havin' a wild crittur in a cage, who oughta be free."

Then the neighbours would glance at each other again, and shift uneasily – because, in their world, not many people used words like 'free'.

But Josh Ferral thought for himself, and spoke as he liked, not turning away from the shadowed fears that lurked just beyond the sameness of village life. He even kept a small store of books, from the Forgotten Time – crumbling and flaking, but enough to give Finn the basics of reading and writing. From the books, and from Josh's store of information passed down by word of mouth over the generations, Finn had added to his education – by learning about the past.

Much of what he learned was disjointed, half-understood, full of puzzles and mysteries. But it was more than most people around him cared to know, or think about, concerning the Forgotten Time, and the horror that came after it.

*

15

It seemed that in the Forgotten Time – long ago, maybe three hundred years or more – the world had been full of people, billions of them. They built huge cities out of metal and stone, spread stone roadways across the land, lived and worked and travelled with always a barrier of stone or metal between them and the outdoors. They lusted after riches and power, those people, and their lust spread poison over the earth and through the air, choked the rivers and oceans, razed the forests and slaughtered wild creatures.

And in the end those people destroyed themselves.

Somehow they set nearly all the world on fire. And afterwards, when the fires died, most of the great cities were blasted ruins, and there were only a few million people left out of all the billions.

Those survivors skulked among the ruins, trying to stay alive, dreaming of rebuilding the world the way it had been. They might even have done so – but they did not have the chance.

No one was sure how long it was – a few generations after the destruction, maybe a century. But one day, without warning, with a terrifying suddenness, vast angular metal shapes appeared in the skies. In their hundreds, they settled slowly on to the ravaged earth.

They had come – on the first day of the world as it now was.

They stalked over the world with cold, alien indifference. They were humanoid, but not human – thin of arm and leg, with torsos bulging like the thoraxes of insects, and small hairless heads that were almost featureless save for a slash of mouth and rectangles of yellow, many-faceted eyes. And the leftovers of the human race fled or hid in howling terror.

But not all. Some bravely tried to learn about the aliens, to make contact with them. They did not succeed. It became clear that a human who got too close to an alien, however innocently, was a dead human. The aliens carried tubular metal staffs from which could blaze deadly, crimson rays of intensified energy. And they used their weapons on humans as casually as a man might kill flies.

Somehow the remnants of the human race gathered their courage, salvaged a few weapons from the wreckage of their civilization, and rose against the invaders. Their defiance lasted only for days. At the first sign of opposition, the alien ships lifted. Human weapons proved useless against their metal bulk, and the ships bore more powerful versions of the energy rays. Coldly, methodically, the aliens set about exterminating humanity.

No human habitation escaped the murderous rays. Even the burnt-out ruins of the old cities were burnt again, melted into oblivion. And as the world went up in flame for a second time, humanity burned with it.

The aliens sent out their weird bat-winged creatures, to spy out where the rebels gathered, for the slaughter. And in the end only a few escaped – perhaps numbering no more than thousands, throughout the world – by fleeing to those regions where the wilderness that they once had shunned now offered them sanctuary.

There they remained, for the aliens, after their total victory, did not bother to pursue the few survivors. But even so, in the face of the aliens' effortless supremacy, and the cold murderousness of the carnage, something had been quenched within the spirit of mankind.

A few still secretly nursed their hatred, but it was an empty, powerless hatred, born of terror and despair. Pride, courage, rebellion, hope – all such feelings were gone from the heart of man. Nothing remained but the blind animal instinct to survive.

*

Yet they did survive, over the years and generations that followed. They re-learned some of the ways of their early ancestors, and lived in an uneasy, primitive co-existence with nature. For nature was recovering herself, spreading the wilderness back over the face of the earth, masking and burying the ghastly scars of two devastations.

As nature reclaimed her world, and sheltered the cowering remnants of humanity, the aliens went about their cold, indifferent, incomprehensible business. They built a few scattered, complex settlements, dotted the land here and there with strange, intricate contrivances, made Earth and all her remaining riches their own.

And no one, still, knew why. There had never been any communication between humans and the earth's new masters. But then, as Josh Ferral had once said to Finn, "People don't waste much talk on mice in the haystacks, neither."

There was no doubt that that was how things were.

The surviving humans made lives for themselves in small, crudely built villages, huddled in the hearts of the spreading, all-encompassing forests. They cleared small fields, and tilled them with primitive implements. And few ever spoke of the aliens, if they could help it. But the awareness of their presence was always there.

Early in the years after the 'rebellion', mankind had learned that there were certain lines that could not be crossed. They learned that they could not build their villages too large, or too close together; and that they could not use what hazy memories they had of science, industry and technology. There was to be no sort of progress back towards anything like the civilization that most of them scarcely remembered.

They learned these lessons by brutal trial and error. The spywings, as the people called the aliens' flying creatures, might visit a village at any time – hovering over roofs and fields, flapping outside windows. If a village had been extending itself, or if someone had re-invented some useful device or process, the spywings would find it. Then the aliens would come, not in one of the great ships but in strange, egg-shaped machines that hovered slightly above the ground. And the energy rays would blaze, and whatever was forbidden would be erased – along with any humans who got in the way.

And there were other, crueller lessons. Sometimes the aliens would come without cause or warning, and people would be taken. The taking seemed to be random – and, as ever, no one knew why, or what happened to those who were taken.

It was the final confirmation of man's new role, on his own planet. Oppressed, degraded, ignorant, afraid, humans were no more than beasts to their alien rulers, 'mice in a haystack', to be ignored and kept under control, or to be tormented and casually killed.

Yet humanity somehow went on surviving. And because fear and hopelessness and despair cannot be confronted every moment, or they will overwhelm the mind, humans learned to push away their thoughts of these things. They learned to let each day's drudgery occupy their bodies and minds, to find what small satisfactions they could in the simple fact of continuing life. They turned their minds and hearts away from vague dreams of freedom, and peace, and happiness, and seldom spoke of such things.

They seldom even spoke, if they could avoid it, the name that men had given, generations before, to their cruel, remote, unfathomable masters.

They had called them . . . the Slavers.

Finn Ferral pulled himself with an effort out of the chill

mists of memory, and looked around the interior of the cabin. All the things that had once simply been 'home', cheery and familiar, now seemed to hold no meaning for him, with Josh and Jena gone . . . Again tears threatened behind his eyes, and a lump swelled in his throat.

But there was another sensation growing deep within him. Something hard as iron, sharp as flint, solid and unshakeable. Determination, perhaps, resolve, containing in it a mixture of wild anger.

If home was no longer home, then he would leave it. He had often dreamed about leaving the village, to search for some answer to the puzzle of his origin. But he had not done so, because there were Josh and Jena to think about – and in any case he had not the slightest idea where to begin looking, or for what.

Josh and Myra had once thought that there might be a clue to his origin in the strange pattern of dark dots, on Finn's left upper arm. But try as they might, they could find no meaning in the pattern – and so eventually concluded that it was just an unusual birthmark.

Unconsciously Finn's fingers rubbed across the mark as he looked around the cabin once more. Then he shook himself like a dog and turned towards the door. The cabin could be left as it was; there was nothing there he needed. And it would be best if things were the same, when he came back. Because he did not plan to wander aimlessly. If he came back, he would not come back alone.

Outside, the crowd had drifted off to their houses, Hocker with them. But the tall man stood in front of Finn's door, looking at him quietly from under bushy brows.

"Finn."

Finn nodded. "Mr. Collis."

"Y' don't want to let Hocker upset y'. What happened cracked his mind open some. He'll get over it."

Finn shrugged indifferently. "Which way did they go?"

Collis blinked, then understood. "North-west," he said, with a jerk of his long chin. "Why? You fixin' t' go after 'em?"

Finn nodded.

Collis blinked again, a fear-glint in his eyes. "They'll kill y'."

Finn shrugged as before, and began to turn away.

"Y're a wrong 'un, fer a fact, boy," Collis said. "Ain't a man alive'd do what y're doin'. They'll kill y' fer sure. Y' can't go up against them."

Finn turned, a wild flare of light in his eyes. "When was the last time anybody tried?"

"An' what about the village?" Collis said. "Who'll do our huntin'?"

"Let Hocker and the others learn," Finn said, smiling without humour. "The wilds won't let you starve. I've got hunting of my own to do, awhile."

Then he turned his back finally on the other man and strode away across the village, towards the north-west.

3

The Pursuit

FINN PLUNGED INTO the forest without looking back towards the village, which was quickly lost from his sight as the greenery closed round him. He moved in a half-crouch, his path zig-zagging from side to side as he searched the uneven ground.

Though he had never before seen one of the vehicles of the Slavers – the 'whirlsleds', as humans called them – he knew a little about them from comments by old Josh. "Like big metal eggs," Josh had described them. "'Cept the top's glass or some such, an' the underside's a bit flat. An' under there they're all spinnin' an' twisty an' hard t' look at. It's like that spinnin' stuff holds 'em up, just a little ways off the ground, so they slide over anythin' slick as you c'd want."

Finn had no idea what it was that kept the vehicles suspended in the air, nor whether a machine riding above the ground would leave any sign of its passage. But he did not want to consider the possibility that the whirlsleds could not be tracked. If some kind of force held the whirlsleds up, he reasoned, that force must leave a mark . . . somewhere, somehow.

So he doggedly continued his sweeping search, moving farther into the forest towards the north-west.

And before long he found what he wanted. Signs of a

sort there were: a tuft of long grass twisted, out of parallel with its shorter neighbours; dust on a patch of bare earth forming a strange whorled pattern; a twig here and there bent or broken, as if by the passage of some heavy body about a metre from the ground.

They were not signs that would have been noticed by most eyes. But to Finn they were like bright flags. They showed him what to look for, gave him a direction, and occurred often enough to let him follow the trail at a run.

And so he ran – a relaxed, loping jogtrot that he could keep up hour upon hour. The trail seemed to be moving straight as a plumb line, except when the whirlsled had had to swing aside briefly to avoid the bulk of a tree or a tangled thicket. Yet Finn did not relax his careful examination of the ground around and ahead. He could not risk losing the trail, if the whirlsled turned on to a different course. And also the fierce concentration helped to keep at bay some of the thoughts and feelings that swarmed like wasps within him.

Dominant among those feelings was pure, chilling fear – rising partly from his own ignorance. When it came down to it, he knew almost nothing about the Slavers. He had never seen one. He had only the general idea that all humans had of what the creatures were, and what they were capable of doing when they came among the villages. Certainly he had no idea what they did elsewhere – where they went, how they lived, what kind of places they had made for themselves.

So he was aware – if he let himself think about it – that he was very probably running straight towards his own death, or captivity. He had not stopped to ask himself what he proposed to do if he caught up with the whirlsled. He did not have the ghost of a plan for wresting Josh and Jena from the aliens.

He merely followed the trail, telling himself that he

would think about these matters when the time came, when he knew more about what kind of situation Josh and Jena were in.

One thing he did know – that both of them, especially little Jena, would be in the grip of a greater terror than he could imagine. When he thought about that, a blaze of anger would sweep through him, drowning his own fear, and he would have to fight against the urge to break into a wild, exhausting sprint.

Now and then, as he kept up his relentless pace, he would pause, to scoop some water from a forest rivulet, to snatch up a handful of wild tubers and chew them for what nourishment they could give. But otherwise he did not pause or even slow his pace, as the day advanced. He simply ran on. It was, he told himself, all there was to do.

The wilderness around him began to change slightly by the late afternoon. From the fairly dense stands of heavy-branched trees, with plenty of rich undergrowth, Finn entered a broad belt of evergreens. Their trunks, soaring many metres above Finn's head, were bare of branches until the very top, where they spread out in a burst of green needles to form a tightly packed canopy.

The breeze drifted through those treetops with a ghostly, whistling sigh, but Finn was not troubled by the eerie sound, nor by the dimness on the forest floor beneath that canopy. The sunlight's inability to penetrate the evergreens meant that the ground was almost bare, save for swathes of light ferns or low flowering plants, and a thick carpeting of dead needles.

And the whirlsled's passage had stirred the needles, leaving them – like the dust, earlier – in strange, coiled whorls. It made a trail that any man could have followed, and that was like a paved highway to Finn.

Yet he did not increase the pace of his easy, loping run. Weariness was gathering in his legs – and the shadowed dimness under the evergreens was growing even dimmer, as the day wore to a close. Soon, in full darkness, he would have to stop, when he could no longer see the trail.

He tried not to think about how far ahead the Slavers might be, or how much distance they would gain if they did not stop for the night.

At least, though, he would have no difficulty picking up the trail again in the morning. Or so he felt – before he reached the clearing.

It was an ordinary patch of open ground, within the stands of tall firs. But the disturbance of the needles and dry earth in the clearing told a story that filled Finn with the sick numbness of despair.

The trail that he had been following had converged with two other exactly similar trails, coming into the clearing from other directions.

Automatically Finn's eyes sorted out the meaning from the chaos of marks and patterns, now barely visible in the gathering darkness. And no matter how he tried to find some other answer, there was none.

Three whirlsleds had entered the clearing, had paused awhile, clustered together, and then had gone their separate ways – one to the north-west, one to the north, one swinging off due westwards.

And there was not the slightest chance that Finn could tell one from another, or know which of the three held Josh and Jena.

Worse, there were faint signs that suggested that some people – or Slavers – had briefly left the sleds during that meeting. Nothing that he could see indicated *why* they had done so. But the possibility existed: there might have been a transfer of prisoners.

He stood motionless, staring at the ground, until he could see it no longer because of the arrival of darkness, and because of the blurring wetness that filled his eyes. At last he turned away, moving with a weary slowness as if the exertions of the day had come upon him all at once. Indifferent to the hunger gnawing at him, he found a hollow at the foot of a nearby tree, and curled into it, wrapping his arms round himself against the growing chill of the night. Eyes closed, he lay motionless. But sleep was a long time coming.

The first grey threads of dawn had scarcely penetrated the canopy of trees, had not yet even awakened a bird, when Finn's eyes opened. He rose at once, stretching catlike to loosen his stiffness after the night's chill, and stepped again into the clearing. For a long moment he stared without moving at the ground, as if hoping to find some different meaning in the disturbed needles.

But there was none. Eventually he raised his head, eyes filled with bleak misery. He had to choose – one chance in three. And it was an obvious choice. The whirlsled he had been following had moved in an unerring line, straight north-west. There was a good chance that the same one would continue in that direction.

Whether it still held Josh and Jena was another question. He would follow it, and find out. It was, he told himself again, all there was to do.

He moved away, again taking up the steady, distance-eating lope that did not waver or slacken. By mid-morning he had moved out of the belt of evergreens, and was moving into an area of parkland – broad expanses of rolling meadow, interspersed with shadowed stands of great trees, like islands in a sea of grass. Once again the whirlsled's path grew difficult to follow, but the faint and minimal signs were there, and were enough for Finn.

He ran on, throughout the day. As before, he paused for moments now and then for a gulp of whatever water the land offered, a mouthful of tough and fibrous roots. Those did little to ease his hunger, but he tried to ignore it – as he tried to ignore the tightness in his legs, the growing ache in his lungs.

By the evening of that day he was moving at a pace not much more than a walk. But he was still moving – until darkness again sent him seeking a place to curl up for the night. And that night, sleep came more swiftly.

Next day, and the next, the pattern repeated itself. Finn now seemed more like quarry than pursuer – like a stag, beset by wolves, who runs and runs until even his powerful legs and great heart give way, and he falls, sweating and foaming, legs twitching as if still trying to carry him to safety. Finn was not driven, like the stag, except by his own determination, and his fears. But he ran during those days with the same wild, mindless, desperate refusal to surrender.

By the end of the fourth day of the pursuit, the land had begun to rise, leading up to a ridge of bare, grassy hills. By then also a chill, lancing rain had begun to fall, making the faint signs even more difficult to see. But still Finn forced himself onward over the uneven ground of the ridge, his chest and legs afire, yet never wavering from the trail.

At one point he fell, partly from his exhaustion, and lay still for a long moment, despite the rain. But at last he forced himself up, stumbling forward even more slowly, to the crest of the ridge. And there he stopped, abruptly, and his weariness fell away as adrenalin flooded through him.

The ground before his feet sloped down steeply into a narrow valley, almost a rift or ravine, since it sloped up again as steeply on the far side. But Finn was no longer looking at the terrain.

The valley was occupied. Two oddly shaped metal

structures, gleaming dully in the rain, reared up from the mud-smeared grass of the valley floor.

Finn slid hastily back into cover. He had seen a few human figures, trudging slowly through the mud round the structures. But he knew very well that this was no human settlement.

He had found a Slaver base.

4

Valley of Fear

KEEPING OUT OF sight, Finn wriggled sideways to where
some low, broad-leaved bushes sprouted near the crest of
the ridge. There he lay motionless behind the cover of the
leaves, oblivious to the rain, staring down into the narrow
valley – trying to make sense of the strangenesses it held,
like nothing he had ever seen before.

In the centre of the valley, rising out of an almost
circular patch of bare, muddy ground, stood an object that
looked as if it were trying, without much success, to
imitate a tree. It was a narrow structure like a spindly
tower, made of greyish metal, angled and jointed along its
length in a way that seemed disturbingly wrong to a
human eye. At its top, giving the vague resemblance to a
tree, was an eruption of slim metal rods, some bent and
contorted, others sprouting still smaller, slimmer rods.

At the foot of the structure, another cluster of heavier
rods thrust out, pushing into the soil like a mockery of
roots. And Finn could see that directly below the tower of
metal the ground had been dug away – or bored into – to
leave a dark pit whose depth he could not guess at.

Beyond the tower and above it, on the steep slope of the
far side of the valley, stood the other structure – larger,
flatter, looking like a box made by someone who did not
use right angles. The end farthest from where Finn lay

rested firmly on – or perhaps *into* – the rocky flank of the steep incline. The other end, jutting straight out from the hillside, was supported on several metal struts reaching down to the slope that fell away below. The struts looked almost too thin to bear the weight, and were also oddly angled, as were the walls of the structure.

Along those walls ran a narrow platform, or walkway. And the walls showed some markings that might have been the seams of openings, in among a weird array of tubes, rods, and bulges jutting here and there from the metal surface.

Two other metal constructions caught Finn's eye. One was an assortment of thin metal posts, standing upright in the ground near the tower, and forming an almost rectangular enclosure. Yet, puzzlingly, they were wide enough apart for a man to pass between, and they enclosed nothing except bare ground.

The other was the flattened-egg shape of a whirlsled, resting silent and empty beside one of the struts that supported the large, box-like structure.

At least he knew what *that* object was. But its familiarity was not at all comforting. Finn felt himself shiver, felt his skin crawl – not from the cold rain that still drove down relentlessly, but from the air of alien menace that surrounded the weird structures.

But he remained still, watching. There were no Slavers in sight, as far as Finn could see from his vantage point. But there were plenty of other living beings moving around the structures. And only some of them were human.

About twenty humans, Finn counted, of various ages and sizes. All were half-naked, in shreds and rags of what had once been clothing. All were filthy, and being made more so by the mud they trudged through as the rain lashed down. Some carried injuries – a dragging foot, an

30

arm hanging limp or clutched to a side, a strip of grimy rag twisted round a head or limb. All were stooped, sagging, slow-moving, blank-faced, as if they were burdened and broken beyond any thought of healing. Finn, his throat tightening with equal mixtures of rage and pity, felt he was looking at the walking dead.

And they would not even have been walking, he knew, if it had not been for the other beings moving among them – like creatures from a nightmare.

They were vaguely human in shape, but as deformed and distorted in their own way as the metal structures were in theirs. Some were short, some tall, but all were heavy-bodied, powerfully built. Most wore a wrapping of dirty cloth over their loins, and a few wore bulky boots. Otherwise all were unclothed – but were covered by dense and matted hair that grew like the pelts of beasts on every part of their bodies.

Finn could not see their faces clearly, past the tangled beards and hair, but glimpses reinforced the impression of beasts – low, jutting brows and brutally coarse features, with now and then a flash of over-large teeth that resembled fangs.

Finn counted a half-dozen of these beast-men. They were clearly the overseers, driving the half-dead humans to their labour. Some of the creatures carried primitive weapons, as ugly as themselves – a knotted club thrust into a waist-band, a long cruel knife. But all of them also held short, thick rods in their hands.

And when a human slipped or stumbled or halted his dazed plodding progress, from one of those rods would burst a thin filament like reddish light, about a metre long. The bestial wielder would lash fiercely with the filament at the offending human – and Finn would hear, over the driving rain, the high, weak wail of agony and despair.

Then every muscle of Finn's body would clench with fury. But still he did not move. He remained on the ridge-top, watching, as the afternoon wore slowly on, as the rain slackened and died away, as the westering sun split the clouds to shed some belated warmth on the scene of torment and horror in the narrow valley.

He watched, and tried to understand. He could see that the humans were simply beasts of burden – many of them occupied with hauling away, in crude baskets, loads of earth and splintered rock dredged up from the pit beneath the tower. Other humans, tended by beast-men, carried stranger burdens – bundles wrapped in gleaming cloth, puzzling tangles of metal – from the box-like structure to the tower, passing them up inside to whoever or whatever awaited them there.

It was clear that, whatever it was, the tower was still under some kind of construction. But hours of watching made Finn no wiser as to its purpose.

Still he could at least guess that the other, larger structure would be some kind of dwelling. The Slavers in the whirl-sled had to have gone somewhere. But it was almost dusk before his guess was confirmed – when one of the door-like panels on the wall of the box-like structure opened like an eye, and a Slaver emerged on to the platform.

Finn hardly breathed as he studied the tall, thin form. The weirdly bulging torso and skinny limbs – the dark, all-of-a-piece covering – the yellow, many-faceted eyes – all were as he had been told. But being told was a far cry from seeing at first-hand. Carefully he studied every centimetre of the monster that was his deadly enemy.

Josh and others had spoken of the heatlance, the long and murderous tube that had burned down so many humans. But this Slaver carried nothing in its three-clawed hands. It seemed that the aliens, totally secure in their own domain, did not feel the need to go armed about the base.

The Slaver's slit-mouth opened. The sound was somewhere between a stream of clicks and a strangled yell. But the beast-men understood. The red filaments flashed in the gathering twilight, herding the humans together, driving them towards the strange enclosure made by the thin, wide-separated posts. Within that space the people huddled, most of them sinking at once to the sodden ground, in postures of exhaustion and total despondency.

As the beast-men then drifted off towards the far side of the box-like building, growling or grunting in low tones among themselves, a second Slaver clambered out of the tower, and stalked towards the box-like structure, disappearing inside.

Even then, when they had passed out of sight, Finn did not move. Not until full darkness had descended on the hillside, bringing with it a damp, cutting wind, did he rise from his hiding place.

Crouching low, so he would not be seen against the skyline, he again stretched the stiffness from his body. No lights showed from either structure – but there were stars enough showing through the wisps of cloud to light the way for Finn's night vision.

He had not seen Josh or Jena among the wretched group of humans. But he had not had a clear look at every one of the downcast, mud-smeared faces. In any case, it was possible that there were other humans elsewhere on the base – perhaps in the larger structure. And there was only one way to find out.

Cautiously, silent as a hunting cat, he moved down the steep incline towards the place of the aliens.

He did not detect the other movement, coming from the larger building. A sweep of small batwings, also silent as a shadow, invisible against the dark sky.

One of the spywings of the Slavers, spiralling upwards to begin an aerial patrol of the valley.

5

Confrontation

FINN HAD BEEN squatting for some minutes just outside
the enclosure before any of the people within it noticed
his still form in the darkness. By then a newly risen moon
had appeared over the farther crest of the ridge, and in its
fitful light through the rags of clouds he was no longer
invisible. A girl saw him first, and shrank away with a
startled gasp. Some others turned to look, and fear swept
vividly across their grimy, drawn faces. Then Finn rose to
his full height, showing himself to be neither beast-man
nor Slaver.

Even then they seemed no less afraid. The idea of a free
human walking loose in a Slaver base was wholly
unknown to them. And what was unknown was terrifying.

"Who be you?" whispered an older man, scrawny and
bent from his labouring. "What y' doin'?"

"I'm—" Finn paused. Somehow he did not want to have
his name known among strangers. "I'm seeking two
people – a man and a young girl. Slavers took them,
maybe brought them here."

The old man moved closer, peering through the
darkness. But it was the girl who had first seen Finn who
replied. "You come lookin' for folk who been taken? You
goin' to help us?"

"'Course he ain't," rasped the old man. "He can't help.

34

Ain't no help for us. Boy's a fool – he'll be dead come sun-up. All us'll be dead if he don't get away from us."

Finn looked at him wonderingly. "You sound like you want to stay here. Why don't you just walk away?"

In reply, the old man picked up a twig and tossed it at the space between two posts. Finn heard a crackling hiss, saw specks of red light dance round the twig, smelled the tang of wood burning. Where the twig had been, ash fluttered to the ground.

"Slavers keep their deathfire 'tween them posts," the old man growled. "Like in the whirlsleds – or the forcewhips them savages use on us. No one c'n walk through there till they turn it off."

Finn blinked, storing the bits of information away. "What about the folk I seek?"

The old man turned away, sinking down to the ground, muttering to himself. The girl answered. "Only one new one come – yesterday, it was. But it was a young fella, name of Lyle. He died."

Finn's heart and breath seemed to stop within him. Not because of the death of young Lyle. He was sorry enough for Hocker's son, but the village and its people seemed far away, from another time. No, he was stricken because it had, after all, been the wrong trail. And the time he had lost . . . the other trails grown cold beyond recall, probably blurred and lost in the wind and rain . . .

Defeat and hopelessness might then have crushed his will, drained his determination. But that most deeply ingrained part of his being that belonged to the wilderness was not affected.

Somehow he sensed a presence, as a wild creature can seem to sense danger with an awareness beyond sight or hearing. He jerked his head up – and the girl's eyes automatically lifted as well.

With her gasp of fright some of the others turned to

35

look, and a soft moan of terror swept the enclosure.

The Slaver spywing, bat-shape silhouetted now in the moonlight, was curving lazily through the night sky towards the huddled group of humans.

"Get away, boy!" the old man hissed. "They'll punish us!"

Finn scarcely heard the words. He had no idea whether the spywing had seen him, or what would happen if it did. But he had already unwrapped the rawhide thong of the sling from around his left wrist, and had plucked a heavy, sharp-edged stone from his belt-pouch. The sling whirled, humming, three times above his head – then released.

He had been bringing down small game with a sling for most of his life, and his accuracy was considered a near-miracle in his village. In an eerie silence the spywing careened in the air, then spiralled down to the ground only a few paces from the enclosure.

Finn stepped towards it for a closer look – and halted, hairs on his neck bristling with shock and fear.

The body of the spywing, no larger than that of a good-sized bat, had been ripped open by the stone. But it was not blood that dripped from the wound – it was a thin, greenish liquid. And it was not flesh and bone that showed within the gaping slash, but the glint of metal.

Even the spywing's eyes – disproportionately large, bulging, many-faceted – were not organic, but something akin to glass.

The old man's voice rasped from behind him. "Dead afore sun-up, that boy. An' us with him, like as not."

But Finn, swiftly rewrapping his sling, paid no attention. His keen hearing had detected muffled sounds from the other side of the building on the far slope. Whether it was because of the spywing, or for some other reason, beast-men were emerging, and were coming round the building.

There was no time to run back up the incline into cover. Instead, Finn leaped *towards* the building, heading for the far corner and the shadows beneath the supporting struts – hoping to circle round the structure and keep it between himself and the approaching beast-men.

But as he gained the darkness under the struts, he heard more sounds from a different direction. Beast-men were coming around *both* sides of the building.

Close to panic, Finn stared wildly around. He was trapped where he was, and he could not trust in the darkness to keep him hidden for long if the beast-men were actually searching for an intruder. Yet he did not stand a chance if he broke away and tried to run, for he had heard enough about Slaver weapons to know how effective they were over distances.

There was only one way to go. Upwards.

Seconds before the first group of beast-men came into view round the corner of the building, Finn clambered up one of the strangely angled struts, reached up to grasp the edge of the narrow platform that ran round the outside of the building, and pulled himself up on to its clammy metal surface.

The group of beast-men passed below him, growling and grumbling among themselves as they were joined by the second group that had come round the building from the other direction.

They were moving towards the enclosure – so likely it *had* been the destruction of the spywing that had brought them out. Finn raised his head cautiously, and counted six of the bulky shapes – all with their backs to him. It was just the chance he needed.

He rose silently to a low crouch, a shadow among the shadows. He was intending to move round the building, on the platform, to the far side where the structure rested against the slope. From there it would be only a short dash up to the top of the slope, and safety.

By the enclosure, the voices of the beast-men rose in a burst of snarling shouts. Obviously they had found the wrecked body of the spywing, and were not pleased. A high-pitched whimper from a human throat indicated that the people in the enclosure knew very well what form the creatures' displeasure would take.

There was nothing that Finn could do now for the imprisoned humans. But compassion and anger made him pause to glance back. With automatic caution, as he did so, he moved back to the wall of the building, flattening himself against it.

But a mechanism that he could not have guessed at was activated by the slight pressure of his back. Without warning a portion of the wall behind him slid smoothly open – and Finn, thrown off balance, stumbled backwards through the opening, into the building.

At once he turned, righting himself. In the space of one heart-beat his eyes swept across the interior of the place. That glance registered the eerie, flat lighting, the angled walls lined with unnervingly alien objects – metal protrusions, rods and tubes, knobs and spheres, screens that flickered with yellow light or buzzed and clicked erratically. In front of the screens, two tall and rounded mushroom shapes jutted from the floor – and these at least Finn recognized as seats.

Because from one of them a Slaver was rising, turning to face him, its terrible yellow eyes darkening through orange and red into an icy purple.

For a frozen moment the two beings stared at each other. Finn was gripped by total, immobilizing terror, and the Slaver seemed held in the same immobility by sheer surprise. Later Finn would come to know that the eyes' colour change registered the emotion – astonishment, turning to anger, as a human might be surprised and

38

outraged to find a mouse in his kitchen.

But then the motionless instant ended. The alien's thin slash of a mouth opened, emitting a rasping series of clicks, and the three-clawed hands snatched at a heatlance that was clipped neatly to the wall nearby.

Panic overcame Finn. Behind him the door had slid closed, and he had not the faintest idea how to reopen it. He could see something that looked like another, inner door, but on the far side of the room, too far away. And the monster in front of him now had its murderous weapon firmly in its grip.

But within a trapped wild animal, no matter how overmatched, panic and terror transform themselves into ferocious, frantic aggression. Finn bared his teeth and leaped unflinchingly straight at the Slaver's throat.

The wild frenzy of the attack took the Slaver off guard. Before it could bring the heatlance to bear, Finn was upon it. His hands grasped the weapon, twisting it fiercely aside, as the momentum of his charge flung the alien crashing back against the screens.

A part of Finn's mind noted that the spindly arms of the Slaver seemed unnaturally weak, offering little resistance as he wrenched the heatlance from its hands. The clawed fingers flailed out, striking at Finn's face, as the eyes' purple grew almost black, and the strangled rattle of clicks from its gaping mouth grew higher in pitch.

Finn evaded the claws, and struck fiercely with one end of the lance against the bulging chest of the alien. But the body seemed solid, as if armoured, and the blow had no effect. Again the claws struck, slashing at Finn's arms, leaving triple streaks of red on his tanned skin.

But then he had shifted his grip, and slammed the sturdy metal of the heatlance, two-handed, across the alien's scrawny throat.

The clicking cry was cut off as Finn forced the ghastly

head farther back. The skinny arms and legs flailed weakly, ineffectually, and the eyes darkened even further. Then there was a metallic snap, and the misshapen body sagged, the head lolling back at a sickening angle on the broken neck.

Cautiously Finn stepped away, panting heavily, aware that his body was drenched in icy sweat. Still unconsciously gripping the heatlance, he stared down at the dead alien. Its eyes had now lost all colour, looking like two rectangular bulges of dirty glass. A trail of thin greenish fluid trickled from one corner of the gaping mouth.

Curiously, Finn prodded the torso with one end of the lance. Despite the flexibility of the spindly arms and legs, the Slaver's upper body was rigid – reminding Finn of the hard, shell-like outer casing of some insects. Remembering what he had seen within the wrecked body of the spywing, Finn wondered. If there were time, he would have been tempted to take his knife to the alien corpse, and see what was to be seen within.

But there was no time.

His sixth sense of danger had already brought him half-way round in a crouching whirl when the ugly snarling filled the room, and a searing, blazing line of pain scorched across his left arm.

Two beast-men, savage faces contorted with fury, were plunging through the inner door to the room, forcewhips crackling an angry scarlet.

6

Devastation

FINN SAW SHOCK and murderous hatred in the reddened
eyes of the beast-man in the lead. The fury of the
creature's snarling was horrible – but it was even more
horrible when, from that fanged mouth, came recognizable human speech.

"Here a worm," the guttural voice said. "He dare come
in here, dare kill a Master!"

"First worm I ever see with guts," growled the second
beast-man.

The first one raised his forcewhip again. "We gon' spill
your guts, worm. Gon' burn 'em out, cut 'em out. You
gon' die in bits, take a *long* time."

Forcewhip hissing, the horror lunged towards Finn.

Finn backed away. He felt no panic now, for he had
faced wild beasts enough in the forest, and these monsters
seemed no more frightening than an angry bear. He
shifted his grip on the heatlance he still held, intending to
use it like a blunt spear, to thrust and jab and keep the
whip-wielder at bay.

But his thumb slid into a shallow groove in the smooth
metal near one end of the tube. The lance-tip crackled,
and a tight beam of energy sprang from the lance, small
points of light dancing within the blaze of crimson.

The first beast-man shrieked as the ray struck. He

staggered backwards, his matted fur erupting into flame, a smoking cavity where the centre of his chest had been.

The second one had time only to snatch with his free hand at the knife in his belt before Finn, maintaining the pressure of his thumb, swung the heatlance. And the creature crumpled, his face a charred ruin, on to the motionless corpse of the first one.

Finn released the pressure of his thumb, wide-eyed at the murderous havoc he had caused. But then his thumb fumbled again for the trigger point, for from just beyond the doorway came the clicking cry of another Slaver.

Again the ray fired, blasting a chunk of molten metal from the doorframe. The Slaver must have wisely retreated, for its next cry was more distant, muffled. Yet there was no doubt that it was summoning reinforcements.

At the edge of his vision Finn caught the movement – the iris-like opening of the outer door. He had only a glimpse of a shaggy body as he wheeled, swinging the heatlance. But the ray stabbed into the empty night air as the beast-man beyond the door ducked back. Finn heard heavy feet moving away along the metal platform – and without hesitation he sprang for the gaping door, seeking the open air, with all the wild creature's hatred of fighting in an enclosed space.

As Finn burst out, the retreating beast-man on the platform swung round, in time to receive the slicing heatray across his upper body. Howling in agony, the creature plunged off the platform, his furred body aflame. And Finn followed, leaping lightly down to the shadowed, welcoming turf.

His eyes were not fully readjusted to the darkness, but still he spotted a moving shadow to one side, and fired again. The blaze of the fiery ray revealed yet another beast-man crouching beside one of the building's supporting struts – but Finn's inexperienced aim had been too hasty, and the ray missed the creature, biting instead deeply into the metal. Even so, the beast-man dodged away, seeking cover, and gave Finn the chance he needed to turn and run.

But his escape was cut off. With a humming rush, around the other corner of the building came the whirlsled of the Slavers.

The moonlight showed Finn the shape of the alien within the transparent upper segment of the egg-shaped vehicle. Wielding the heatlance more confidently, he took aim and fired. But the ray glanced harmlessly off the sled's surface. And from a projecting rod at the sled's nose, an answering ray scorched only centimetres past Finn's cheek.

He flung himself aside, falling, scrambling quickly to his feet. He fired twice more as he moved, but again the blasts had no effect on the whirlsled. And again, the sled's weapon cut livid lines of scarlet through the air around Finn, as he dodged and retreated.

The sled was now edging forward slowly, as if its driver intended to get Finn in its sights and keep him there. And Finn knew that the remaining beast-men were moving through the darkness under the building's supports, seeking to attack him from the side.

But still he fought, twisting, weaving and firing, an elusive retreating shadow. Another beast-man shrieked and fell, beneath the struts of the building, as Finn's sweeping heatlance slashed across its legs. Yet the whirlsled was still creeping grimly forward – and Finn knew that the uneven battle could only end one way. Even so, he fought on, a wild fury in him that would keep him fighting until the last breath left his body.

Still moving backwards, his foot struck a patch of wet mud in the darkness, and he slipped, half-falling to one knee.

In that instant the two remaining beast-men sprang from the darkness, and at the same time the whirlsled surged forward towards him, the sudden acceleration lifting it more than a metre from the ground.

Frantically, Finn fired. But he was off-balance, and instead of blasting the beast-men at whom he was aiming, the heatray struck the exposed underside of the sled, just at the place where the smooth metal side curved into the cloud of crackling, sparkling energy on which the vehicle rode.

And the whirlsled veered and lurched, out of control.

Still accelerating, it swung crazily to one side. The two beast-men sprang back as the machine hurtled directly towards them, juddering and twisting, then smashed with an echoing impact into one of the supporting struts of the building – the strut that had been damaged, moments before, by Finn's heatlance.

The whirlsled vanished in a deafening eruption of flame. And the damaged strut cracked across, where it had been weakened, and collapsed.

Slowly at first, then more swiftly, the building began to sag. Metal shrieked under intolerable stresses as the remaining struts took the displaced weight of the building. The struts began to bend, and crumple.

Finn saw the shadowed outline of the two beast-men leaping out from under the building, risking his heatlance in their desperation. But they did not make it.

The struts gave way. With a grinding, splintering roar, the building lurched forward and crashed down. Beast-men and the ruins of the whirlsled were lost to sight as the vast weight descended upon them.

Then Finn too flung himself backwards, scrambling away to safety. For as the metal bulk of the building struck the ground, with its far side still held up on the higher slope, it began to slide. Majestically, unstoppably, like some mighty metal avalanche, it thundered down the slippery, rain-sodden grass and mud of the incline. Narrowly missing the enclosure where the terrified humans cowered and screamed, the building plunged on a straight line towards where the alien shape of the tower reared into the darkness.

It reached the edge of the pit beneath the tower, and toppled over the edge in a rending fury of crumpled, twisted metal. The tower collapsed in upon itself like paper. Flame licked up out of the pit, then erupted in orange tongues higher than the tower had stood. And the explosion that accompanied the flame was the loudest noise Finn had ever heard in his life.

At last stillness returned to the valley. Flames still spat here and there within the pit, but otherwise there was no movement. Nor was there movement on the scarred hillside where the box-like building had stood.

Finn stared around, unmoving, hardly able to believe what had happened, hardly able to grasp the fact that he was alive, and victorious. But he had learned much from that brief and savage battle. He had learned above all that the Slavers and their creatures and machines could be fought – and defeated.

He was aware that he had much thinking to do about what he had learned, for every piece of knowledge seemed to bring with it a hundred more unanswerable questions. But the fact was there – he had confronted Slavers, had fought them, and had survived.

Slowly he stooped to pick up a twig, and walked quietly over to where the human prisoners still huddled, whimpering, in their enclosure. He threw the twig, and watched it sail harmlessly between the posts. Whatever the 'deathfire' was, it was no longer active.

"You're free," he told them simply.

"Free?" It was the voice of the old man again. "We're *dead*, us."

45

But some of the others rose wonderingly to their feet, to edge fearfully between the posts and out of the enclosure. Some went to stare into the pit, shaking their heads and murmuring in low voices. The girl who had spoken to Finn before came to stand near him, looking at him curiously.

"How many Slavers were here?" Finn asked her.

She thought for a moment, then held up two fingers.

"And how many of the hairy ones?"

This time she did not need to pause, but held up six fingers.

"Then we're safe," Finn said. "They're dead – all of them."

"So're us, boy," said the old man dully, stepping forward from the group that still huddled fearfully together near the enclosure. "Or as good as when more Slavers come."

Finn was startled. "They won't find you. Run, now, far as you can. The forest will hide you. The forest is no friend to Slavers."

The old man spat. "Wilds'll kill us as quick as Slavers. Can't live there. Ain't huntsmen, us." Behind him, some of the others muttered agreement.

"Learn to be!" Finn snapped. "What else? Wait here for Slavers and their beasts to come and burn you? Run! Learn! There's life in the forest!"

"We c'd live there," the girl said suddenly, "if we had a huntsman with us, t' show us how. You come with us. Teach us."

Finn shook his head. "I can't. I must find my people. That's the hunting I must do."

"Them folks'll be dead now, or worse," the girl persisted. "You'll maybe never find 'em – or if y' do, y' won't be able t' help 'em. Help us, instead."

"I can't. I have to go my way, make my search. Whatever I find at the end of it."

46

"Go on, then," the old man rasped. "But y've killed us now, boy, sure's if y' took y'r knife to us."

"I haven't killed you," Finn said quietly. "You were as good as dead before I got here. In that." He gestured towards the enclosure.

"And if you can't find life for yourselves in the forest, *free*," Finn went on, his eyes hardening, "why, then – you were as good as dead before *you* got here."

And he turned on his heel and left them where they stood. Nor did he look back once as he sprang up the slope, out of the valley, and the darkness closed off all sight of them.

PART TWO

The Bloodkin

7

The Intruder

FINN LAY ON his belly on a grassy bank overlooking a pool
of clear water, formed by the wandering of a brook
through the forest. In one hand he held a slim pole, a
sapling that he had cut and trimmed. He had split the
thicker end of the pole and jammed the hilt of his knife
into the split, binding it tightly with the leather thong of
his sling. It made a crude spear – but an effective one,
as proved by the two good-sized fish on the grass beside
him.

But he was very hungry, and two fish, once cleaned,
might not be enough. So he remained, staring at the water
unblinkingly, the spear poised. An underwater shadow
flickered, moving erratically towards Finn's side of the
pool. Still he did not move an eyelash – and then the spear
became a blur, driving into the water. It emerged with the
flapping shape of a fish transfixed on the blade. Not a
large one, Finn saw, but it would do.

He pulled the blade free, set the fish down with the
others, and took the spear apart, spreading the sling out
on the grass to dry. Then he went to work on the fish,
tossing the heads and guts back into the pool. Behind him,
a small fire of dry branches burned almost smokelessly in
a shallow pit that he had scooped in the turf. In a few
moments the fire would be a basin of richly glowing coals

– and nearby lay a narrow lattice-work of green twigs, to be placed above the coals like a grill.

In less than a minute the neatly filleted fish lay in place over the fire, already beginning to sizzle. Finn sat back peacefully watching the coals, enjoying the setting sun on his back, seeming wholly absorbed and relaxed.

But his mind was far from peaceful.

Several days had passed since he had turned his back on the chaotic wreckage of the Slaver base, and on the people who seemed to fear freedom as much as captivity. Then, without pause, he had retraced his steps to the clearing in the midst of the evergreen forest, where the three Slaver whirlsleds had met and parted.

He was well aware of how unlikely it was, after the storm of rain, that he would be able to pick up either of the other two trails. And even if he could, he knew he might choose the wrong one, and waste days or even weeks before discovering his error. Yet there was nothing else he could do. Josh and Jena had to have been in *one* of the other two whirlsleds, and he could only pursue one at a time.

Back at the clearing, then, as the sun shed a dim light through the evergreens, he had unhesitatingly made his choice – to follow the sled that had set off almost due west. He had found one or two faint and blurred signs, at widely spaced spots on the carpet of needles – and they had given him a vague, general bearing. So he had gone westwards.

He knew at least that the Slavers tended to drive their vehicles in nearly straight lines. He was counting on that tendency, hoping that he might pick up a clearer trail farther away. So he travelled as before, sweeping in a zig-zag line back and forth across the line of the bearing he had taken, studying the ground with such intensity that scarcely a leaf or a grassblade escaped his scrutiny.

For days he had travelled west in that fashion. He was no longer running with the frantic urgency of his first pursuit, for he knew there was no point in crippling himself with exhaustion. He had no idea how long his search might take, how far he might need to go. So he travelled wisely, forcing himself – though he deeply begrudged the time lost – to find food for a substantial meal at the end of each day.

But as the days passed, Finn had grown more and more desperate. Despite his skills and his unwavering concentration, he had found not a single sign to show that anything like a whirlsled had passed through the forest on the course he was following.

Even if he was pursuing the right whirlsled, he had lost the trail.

Several times a day, as frustration and misery rose within him like a sickness, he had fought the urge to run wildly through the forest, on either side of the line he had chosen, hoping that some lucky chance might let him stumble on the signs he yearned for. But he knew that such an action would be useless. Luck had little to do with forest tracking.

His only hope was to cling to the straight line of the original bearing, and see if it took him anywhere. If not to a Slaver base, then perhaps to a human village, where he might learn if there were Slavers in the vicinity. It was a slim hope, but it was all he had.

And because it was such a slim hope, the end of each day was always a bad time. While travelling, his concentrated study of the terrain left little mental energy for brooding over the painful fact of his loss and his failure. But when he stopped, the awareness flooded in: the knowledge that he had lost the trail, the dreadful thought of what Josh and Jena might be suffering at that very moment. If they still lived . . .

Finn ground his teeth and shook himself, trying to fight off the black thoughts, the mind-numbing sense of hopelessness that they brought. Leaning forward, he flipped the fish over with his knife, tossed a few dry scraps of twigs on to the coals. The fish smelled wonderful, but if he succumbed to the despair that threatened him each evening, he knew they would taste like ashes in his mouth.

He settled back – and then went still, as if turned to stone.

Something was moving in the forest, beyond the brook. Something large, for the sound of rustling branches and crunching twigs indicated a creature big and fearless enough not to have to care much about being silent.

Finn cocked his head, listening, pinpointing the sounds. He was alert and cautious, but not troubled. The forest was well populated with animals, as he knew, including large ones: he had seen several territorial markings of bears on the tree trunks. And this sounded like a bear, perhaps drawn by the fragrance of the broiling fish.

No doubt it would come close enough to have a good sniff, and to inspect Finn. It might even stay around, to see if it could steal some food when Finn slept. As long as Finn kept himself to himself, and presented no danger, the bear would be no danger to him.

Even so, because it is sensible to be cautious in the wilderness, he reached over towards the heatlance that lay nearby, drawing it closer.

He had brought the weapon with him, from the Slavers' valley. Each evening since, he had studied it and practised with it – not that it took any great skill to aim the deadly, scorching ray. So far, though, he had used it only for practising, and as a quick way to ignite a fire. When he hunted for his evening meal, he used his own weapons, feeling somehow that it would be wrong, unnatural, to use the alien weapon on creatures of the wilds.

The bear, or whatever it was, had drawn closer now, moving in a semi-circle around the small pond. Pulling his fish, now cooked, off the fire, Finn set them aside to cool a little, and kept a careful watch on the foliage in the direction of the sounds.

There – a bush trembled slightly. Finn did not look directly at it, but kept it in view from the corner of his eye as he leaned forward to pick up one of the fish.

As he did so, the creature that had been moving so noisily among the trees emerged into full view from behind the bush.

Not a bear. Not any other kind of animal.

It was the bulky, half-naked shape of a beast-man of the Slavers – with a glare that seemed to mingle both surprise and fury in its shadowed, deep-set eyes.

For an instant Finn was rigid with shock. And the beast-man also remained still, studying Finn.

The creature was not tall, but was enormously broad and powerful, stooping slightly, with a jutting hump of muscle on its upper back just below the thick neck. It wore baggy leggings and heavy, knee-high boots, and a long-bladed weapon like a machete was strapped in a leather sheath at its back, the hilt thrusting up above a massive shoulder. The naked upper body was covered with long, shaggy hair that was light in colour, almost yellow, and the face was mostly hidden in a massive dark beard. The heavy jut of the eyebrows made the eyesockets seem like caves, yet the forehead was oddly high, seeming more so because the hair on the creature's head was thinning and receding.

And that forehead was furrowed deeply, as the creature took a wary step forward.

Finn, scrambling up, brought the heatlance with him. The beast-man's eyes widened as it saw the weapon. It halted, crouching as if to leap back. And Finn raised the

54

lance, his thumb stabbing at the shallow groove that fired it.

The tip of the metal rod glowed scarlet. But there was nothing more. No lethal ray of heat flared out.

Frantically Finn glanced down, jabbing again and again at the firing groove. Still nothing. And whatever was wrong with the weapon, it was too late for Finn to discover it.

With surprising speed for a creature of its bulk, the beast-man swept the machete from the sheath at its back. The cruel blade glittered as the creature lunged forward, mouth agape in a bestial snarl.

Finn's knife still lay on the grass, beside the fire, and there was no time for the sling. Gripping the useless lance like a club, he crouched, bracing himself to meet the monstrous charge. They came together like two savage beasts – Finn with the quick and agile ferocity of a cougar, the beast-man with the bulk and power of a maddened bear.

The machete hissed in a looping swing at Finn's head, then clanged resoundingly as Finn struck the blow aside with the heatlance. Again the machete slashed down, seeming weightless in the beast-man's great fist. Finn ducked aside, swinging the lance in a counter-blow that grazed the beast-man's ribs.

So they fenced, stroke and counter-stroke, with Finn mostly on the defensive against the murderous blade of the machete. Several times that deadly edge nicked Finn's jerkin, slicing into the tough leather as if it were paper. But more often Finn remained quick enough to stay out of reach of the flashing blade. And some of his blows found their marks, too – though the solid thump of the lance against the beast-man's belly or leg seemed to have no effect whatever.

The fight lasted only moments, as the two circled,

swayed and struck. It was the beast-man who changed tactics first. A chopping blow at Finn's side became a feint, followed by a crushing kick. But Finn dodged the huge boot, and lashed out fiercely with the lance at the hand that held the machete.

Metal struck a hairy wrist, and the beast-man bellowed as the machete flew from its grasp. Swift as a striking snake, Finn swung the lance around, aiming for his opponent's head. But the beast-man's speed had not been impaired. A vast hand flashed up, clutched the lance – and with awesome, easy power wrenched it from Finn's grasp and flung it away.

Then the monster lunged at Finn's throat.

Like a crazed wildcat Finn fought, with fists and knees and feet. Some of his blows brought deep grunts, but otherwise had no more effect on the beast-man than they would have had on the bole of a tree. The terrible hands gripped Finn's jerkin, dragging him off balance. Locked together in combat, the two toppled to the ground – Finn beneath the beast-man.

All the breath was driven from Finn's lungs by the impact, with the beast-man's enormous weight crushing him. Half-stunned, he could only writhe and twist helplessly as mighty hands and knees pinned him firmly to the ground.

At last he let his body sag, knowing there was no escape, and stared up at the bestial face, waiting for death.

But to his surprise, there was no look of triumph or brutal murderousness on the beast-man's face. Instead, there was something oddly like a crooked smile on the beard-veiled mouth, and something like a twinkle in the deep-set eyes.

"Now then."

Finn blinked in surprise. The beast-man's voice was not like the snarling, barking sound of the others of his kind that Finn had fought. It was deep and rich, rolling like melodious thunder from the depths of the great barrel chest.

"Now then," the creature repeated. "If you're all through tryin' to kill me, maybe we can have ourselves a little conversation."

8

Baer

FINN FELT HIS jaw drop open foolishly. And the beast-man grinned, revealing not fangs but quite ordinary human teeth, if a little large and yellowish.

"Seein' you with that heatlance put the wind right up me," he said. It sounded to Finn almost like an apology. "Guess I kinda lost my head – an' set out to separate you from *your* head." A deep rumbling chuckle. "So that sorta makes us even. Now, if I let you up, you goin' to sit·still an' be good, so's we can talk awhile? You *can* talk, can't you?"

Finn blinked several times, as if not sure all this was really happening, and found his voice. "Yes," he said hoarsely.

"To both questions?" grinned the beast-man. "Good enough."

He released Finn and stood up, backing away with a wariness that belied the grin. Finn lifted himself to a sitting position, half-dazed with astonishment, rubbing at the bruises that the beast-man's great hands had made on his flesh.

He tensed briefly as the man moved to where his machete lay, but the weapon slid back neatly into the sheath on the broad back. Then the beast-man reached down to gather up the heatlance. He did something with his hands, and to Finn's further surprise the lance fell neatly into two halves. The beast-man squinted into the interior of the tube.

"Charge run out," he said. "An' just as well, for me. Got any spares?"

Finn looked puzzled, and shook his head.

"That figures. You find it somewheres?"

Slightly stung, Finn found his voice again. "I took it. From Slavers."

"That so?" The deep-set eyes studied Finn with new interest. "An' what happened to the Slavers?"

"Dead," Finn said, with a faint tinge of pride. "Two of them – and six of their . . . of the others."

A smile of grim approval spread over the bearded face. "Now that's what I like to hear." He paused as a thought struck him. "You have anythin' to do with a ruckus I heard a while back, lots of smoke an' fire, some days' travel over that way?" He pointed in the direction of the valley where Finn had fought his explosive battle.

Finn nodded. "It was a Slaver place – two big things like buildings. They blew up."

"That figures," the beast-man said again. "I was near enough to see that somethin' lively was goin' on." He was still studying Finn carefully. "You're somethin' new to me, boy. Never knew any of your kind who'd raise a hand against the Slavers. An' I sure never saw any who could do it an' come out alive."

Finn reddened slightly. "I'm not sure I knew much about what was happening, some of the time. I was lucky."

"Yep, luck helps if you've got it," the beast-man said amiably. "But you got to be smart an' tough, too, to fight the Slavers. Seems to me you got that as well." The crooked grin flashed again. "I already found out you're stronger'n you look."

59

Finn found himself feeling oddly pleased by the words of praise.

The beast-man lumbered forward, thrusting out a huge hand. "Let's us shake hands, boy, an' be easy with each other. Looks like we're on the same side of things. What's your name?"

"Finn Ferral," Finn said, tentatively holding out a hand – to be effortlessly pulled to his feet by that hand, which was then shaken vigorously.

"Call me Baer," the beast-man said – and then his eyes twinkled as he saw Finn trying to quell a smile. "What's the joke?"

"No offence," Finn said, still striving to keep the smile at bay, "but I . . . I thought you *were* a bear, when I heard you first. And then seeing you, I . . . uh . . ."

"Thought I look like one, too?" Baer said with a chuckle. "That figures. An' you heard me comin', did you? When I thought I was bein' all quiet an' careful." He shook his great head ruefully. "Never did get on too happy in this dam' forest. But now you, Finn Ferral, you seem to get on real good."

"I was huntsman for my village," Finn said simply. "The forest is home to me."

"That so?" Baer said interestedly. He poked at something on the ground, with the toe of his boot, and Finn saw that it was a few shreds of cooked fish, trampled into the turf during their wild fight. "You sure seem to find some good eatin'," Baer went on. "Me, I haven't had my belly full for as long's I like to remember. You reckon there's more fish where these came from?"

Finn was taken aback. Food was the last thing on his mind just then. "There's plenty for the catching," he said, gesturing towards the pool. "But . . ."

"I know," Baer broke in, holding up a hand. "You're all fired up with questions – an' I got as much curiosity 'bout you as you got 'bout me. But my head says we got all night for talkin', an' only a while left 'fore it's too dark for fishin'. An' my belly says I could talk a lot more sense if it got itself filled up, first.''

Finn glanced around. The sun was nearly down, and the shadows were increasingly long. "All right, I'll get some supper. And the fire could do with some building up.''

"That I can do, young Finn,'' Baer rumbled. "If there's two things ol' Baer *can* do – '' he patted the hilt of his machete meaningfully – "it's choppin' firewood, an' killin' Slavers.''

With those grim words echoing around him, Finn turned back to the pool, his mind awhirl with bewilderment and a sense of unreality stirred up by his strange supper guest.

Full darkness had gathered around them for some time before they finished eating. Finn had brought a small mountain of fish back to the fire, and had watched with amazement as Baer chewed his way tirelessly through most of them. While they ate, Finn – on Baer's invitation – had talked about himself. And Baer was a wonderful listener: hunched slightly forward over the fire, gazing at Finn intently as if not to miss a word, giving deep grunts and growls of understanding, approval, sympathy. Finn had found himself pouring everything out, even the details as he knew them of his strange arrival in the village, as well as the more recent events leading up to his frantic pursuit of the whirlsled, and the terrifying confrontation in the valley.

When his story finally wound down, there was a long moment of silence broken only by the sound of Baer's large teeth steadily munching fish.

"Now that,'' Baer said at last, "is what I call a tale

worth tellin'. As good for listenin' to as this fish is for eatin'.'"

Finn shook his head wonderingly. "I still can't believe all this is happening," he said. "A while back I was fighting for my life against . . . what I thought was one of the Slavers' monsters. Now I'm sitting here with him, eating fish and telling all about myself."

Baer nodded, unperturbed. "Does sound funny, put like that. But I've not been one of the Slavers' monsters, like you say, for many a long year."

"Then it's your turn," Finn said, "to tell who you are, and what you're doing here."

"Me, I'm just Baer. An' what I'm doin' is what I been doin' for years. Wanderin', stayin' alive as best I can." The voice deepened further into a rumble like distant thunder. "An' killin' Slavers."

"Why?" Finn asked intently.

"You know why. 'Cause *they're* the monsters. 'Cause it's the only way – you kill them, or they kill you. They been killin' people for more years'n I can count."

"But you're not . . ." Finn stopped, covered with confusion.

"Not people? Not *human*?" Baer's eyes glittered in the firelight. "Maybe I don't look it. Maybe others like me that you've met didn't look it nor act it neither. But we are. From good human stock, just like you."

"I don't understand," Finn began.

"That figures," Baer said. "How could you? Your people, they huddle in their villages an' keep their eyes tight closed, hopin' the bogey man'll go away an' not bother 'em. Too scared to stand up for themselves – too scared even to find out anythin' about the enemy that might *help* 'em stand up. All of 'em – scared an' ignorant." He glanced at Finn with his lopsided smile. "'Cept ol' Baer. An' 'cept you too, now, I reckon."

Finn looked doubtful. "I'm as scared and ignorant as any of them. I've seen the Slavers, and fought them, and all I know now is how much I don't know. And I *need* to know."

Baer tossed the clean bones of the last fish on the fire, and leaned back with a satisfied belch. "Yep, you do, or you won't live out the month. An' ol' Baer's just the fella to teach you. Like you say, it's my turn for story-tellin'." Again the lopsided smile. "But don't go complainin' if what I tell you gives you a month's worth of nightmares."

Baer proved to be as good a talker as he was a listener. As the night wore on, and the moon shed an edge of silver on to the shadows around the red-glowing fire, Finn sat motionless, scarcely seeming to breathe, as if hypnotized by the rolling bass melody of Baer's voice. Yet he was listening with total absorption, not missing a word.

Baer began with himself. "We'll start small," he said with his crooked grin, "an' get to the state of the world later on." He had indeed been born and raised as 'one of the Slavers' monsters', in a Slaver centre far to the west, within a range of great mountains. It was one of the main centres, he told Finn, maybe the biggest of all, covering a large area and with a sizeable population.

Like all the others of his kind, Baer went on, he had served the 'masters' as required. When he reached his full growth, he joined his fellows in the task of guarding – or herding – the extensive collection of human slaves at the centre. But the fact that Baer did his duty did not prevent him from seeing how hopeless and helpless the people were.

He watched them stumbling through their labours, like the beasts of burden that they had become. He watched them being tormented and cruelly driven by the beast-men

– including himself. He watched them weaken and die, with terrible swiftness, to be replaced by others just as hopeless, wretched and doomed.

But from the beginning, Baer had known that there was something different about himself, setting him apart from the others of his savage kind. Perhaps it was a higher level of intelligence; perhaps an edge of compassion awoke in his nature. Whatever it was, he found himself feeling sorry for the human slaves. And he found himself asking the question that no one asked. The question – *why?*

He also found that the question festered within him until he sought an answer. As best he could, secretly, furtively, he began to study the Slavers.

Over the years he watched, listened, learned, stored information away – piecing it together slowly, building up a detailed picture of who and what the Slavers were, why they had come to Earth, what their long-term plans were. No one seemed to notice that Baer's attitude had changed; no one guessed for a moment what he was doing.

"So I got careless," Baer growled to Finn. "I took chances, sneakin' into parts of the centre where my kind didn't go. I found out a lotta things. An' I also got caught."

For his crime of trespassing into forbidden areas, the Slavers had ordered him killed. And the beast-men, his brothers and comrades, decided for the fun of it to beat him to death slowly, with their forcewhips.

"When they finished, they chucked me down the mountainside, where they threw their garbage." Baer's voice had grown as deep and sombre as a funeral knell. "But I fooled 'em. I wasn't dead. I lay there for days with my wounds turnin' rotten – nothin' to eat or drink, not movin', just hurtin'. But I didn't die. An' a time came when I could move a little, an' scavenge in the garbage for a scrap of food. Later, when the wounds were healin', I

64

crawled off into the wilds, where I been ever since."

But even when Baer was fully healed, there were inner scars, he made clear to Finn, that were never going to heal. They had bred a deep-rooted hatred and anger, a savage desire to strike back. It had been the only thing that had kept him alive as he had lain bleeding into the garbage.

"So I declared war on the Slavers," he rumbled. "Sounds kinda funny – ol' Baer all alone, declarin' war on a whole race of critturs with all their fancy weapons an' machines. But I knew 'em. I knew their weaknesses, their blind spots. I knew how to keep myself safe from 'em, an' how to kill 'em. An' that's what I been doin', ever since. That's what I'll be doin' up to when I take my last breath. Killin' Slavers."

"And your . . . your own kind?" Finn asked hesitantly.

"Yep. Can't kill the one without goin' through the other. But I don't see 'em as my kind any more. They think of themselves as, y'know, kind of a separate breed. Call themselves the *Bloodkin* – like they're all blood-brothers. All they know is doin' what the Slavers tell 'em – an' doin' it as vicious an' ugly as they know how. Me, I think of myself as human, even though most humans'd run a mile if they set eye on me."

Finn frowned. "But how did you . . . how did they get the way they are? Where do they come from?"

Baer gazed at him for a moment. And his reply, which Finn only half-understood, was all the more disturbing for being spoken so calmly.

"Why, we're *made*, boy. Bred special – by the Slavers."

Then Baer grinned his crooked grin at the sight of Finn's thunderstruck face. "Don't get the wrong idea, now. I don't mean we're made like they make their machines, or those bat-critturs. Bloodkin're ordinary flesh an' bone, like you. Come from human folks – born like

65

anybody gets born. Only – 'fore they're born, 'fore they're much bigger'n a pinhead in their ma's belly, Slavers take 'em out. An' do things to 'em."

Appalled, Finn listened to the description of the huge Slaver laboratories that Baer had found in the centre. There the human embryos, no more than fertilized egg cells, were operated on with strange and delicate instruments. After doing whatever was done, the Slavers then replaced the cells, in the wombs of the human mothers, to grow naturally towards birth.

Except, Baer added, many did not survive till birth, or for long afterwards. And those that did were not truly human.

"Some're all twisted an' deformed an' worse," Baer said, "an' the Slavers have 'em killed. Most of the rest come out lookin' like me – and the Bloodkin get a few new boys."

"Boys?" Finn asked.

Baer spat into the fire. "Slavers like the Bloodkin to be big an' strong an' nasty. They kill the girls."

Finn stared unseeingly into the darkness, trying to understand a depth of callous cruelty that he could barely imagine. And then an even more horrifying thought struck him.

"Baer," he began hoarsely, "the mothers . . ."

"Young women, from the people the Slavers take," Baer said. "Bloodkin force 'em to mate with male slaves." The deep voice softened. "I know what you're thinkin', Finn, an' it's prob'ly right. Somethin' you gotta face. Right now, your little sister might be becomin' a mother to one of the Bloodkin."

"No!" The cry seemed to be torn from Finn's throat, as the agony of the thought flooded through him. He glared at Baer, vision blurred. "Why does this happen? *Why?*"

"Dunno for sure, son," Baer said gently. "Slavers don't

explain themselves to Bloodkin. But it always seemed to me that they were tryin' for somethin' special. Tryin' to make a new kind of human. An' I figure the Bloodkin're more an accident, though Slavers find a use for us."

"Then what kind of people do they want?" Finn asked.

Baer began to reply, but stopped abruptly, as if something had suddenly struck him. When he did speak, his voice sounded almost too casual. "Can't tell you, Finn. No way of knowin'."

Half-lost in his own tormented thoughts, Finn did not notice the pause, or the altered tone. Nor did he notice that Baer's eyes had shifted, his gaze sliding across the pattern of small dark dots on Finn's upper left arm.

9

Two Travellers

FOR MANY LONG minutes Finn sat as he was, motionless as a statue, staring into nothingness, lost in thoughts and visions that verged upon the unbearable. At last Baer shifted uneasily.

"Don't let it tear you apart, Finn," he growled. "I know it's hard. But it's a hard an' ugly world. Has been ever since the Slavers came. Can't change that."

Finn turned his gaze slowly towards Baer, his eyes regaining their focus. The firelight cast its shadows upwards across the planes of his face, making them look like they were carved from granite.

"I'll change some of it." His voice was harsh and bleak. "If it kills me. I'm getting Josh and Jena out, wherever they are."

Baer tugged at his beard, scowling. "It's near sure to kill you, boy. If you can find 'em at all. But dam' if I don't feel like followin' along, if you'll have me."

Finn looked at him with surprise. "Why?"

Baer shrugged. "'Cause I got nothin' else to do. 'Cause I'm curious to see how you make out. 'Cause maybe you could do with somebody around who's used to killin' Slavers." A ghost of his crooked smile showed through his beard. "'Cause I near starved to death a few times, an' you seem to eat pretty good."

Finn's expression did not change as he considered the idea. Finally he nodded. "Why not? As long as you don't slow me up."

"I can move pretty good when I get goin'," Baer growled.

"Then we'll set out at first light. And as we go," Finn added, as almost an afterthought, "you can tell me a few more things I need to know. About Slavers – and how to fight them."

By the end of the next day's travel, Finn had no cause for complaint. Baer seemed tireless. For much of the day the course that Finn was following took them across a broad swathe of lowlands, wet and marshy, where the undergrowth spread itself in a lush and tangled barrier. As ever, Finn found gaps and pathways that hardly seemed to exist before he entered them, so it looked as if the tangle was parting to allow him through. Baer did not have this ability, but made up for the lack with his sheer power and stamina, crashing through the jungle-like growth where he could, in a last resort swinging the razor-edged machete to carve openings for his bulk.

They spoke little during the day – for Finn, as usual, ranged widely on either side of the direct bearing he was following, still hoping to pick up some sign of whirlsleds having passed that way. But for his part Baer stayed as near to the straight line of travel as he could, once Finn had indicated it. And when the first fingers of twilight began to reach across the land, they had made a considerable distance.

Finn did not, for once, begrudge the need to turn aside from the day's march and hunt for food. He was looking forward to the evening's talk. It had been a day for thought, when Finn had struggled to come to terms with the ghastly revelations of the night before, and the fate that had probably overtaken Jena. But he also thought about how valuable Baer's company could be, as a source of information about the enemy.

So his head was buzzing with questions. And that night, after they had stuffed themselves to bursting point with the roast meat of some water rodents that Finn had snared, he pressed Baer for answers.

Baer sat back, scratching his beard, as willing as ever to talk. "You got to remember," he began, "that Slavers don't make much conversation, not even to each other. The Bloodkin get orders, but don't ask questions. So there's a lotta things I never figured out."

One things he failed to learn was the origin of the Slavers – what other world they came from. But to Finn, who knew nothing of space travel or other planets, it was a meaningless question. He was far more interested in something Baer *had* found out – what it was that had brought the Slavers to Earth.

"They're dead set on metals," Baer told him. It seemed that most of the smaller Slaver bases were built on or near some source of special metals, left from the Forgotten Time. Not natural ores, but metal that had been worked, or created, by the ancient humans who had built that glittering and unnatural civilization, and then had destroyed it.

"There's lots of that stuff around," Baer went on, "only the wilds've covered it, an' you gotta dig some to get at it. That's what the Slavers do, a lotta the time – dig. Usin' their machines, or their slaves, or both."

It was probably the beginning of one such mining operation, Baer thought, that Finn had stumbled on in the valley.

Baer talked further about leftovers from the Forgotten Time that he had seen. Vast areas that had been so devastated in the final holocaust that the wilderness could make no headway there – and that even Slavers kept away from. In those areas, what sparse plants did grow were weirdly misshapen and often poisonous, and the creatures that roamed those scarred regions were just as malformed and even more lethal.

These tales interested Finn, but not as much as the details that Baer related about the Slavers. How he had never seen them eat, and suspected that they did not sleep, though they kept themselves apart from the Blood-kin at night, so Baer could not be sure. How the colour changes of their eyes did show that they had feelings – but a very limited range, little more than momentary surprise or anger. How those many-faceted eyes also had special abilities to see things that were too small or too distant for the human eye, and to see perfectly well in near-total darkness.

But Finn grew especially intent when Baer spoke of the Slavers' weaknesses. "Those skinny arms an' legs got almost no strength," he rumbled. "The neck's the same." Finn nodded grimly – he had personal knowledge of that fact. "But the bodies – there's nothin' can get through that armour. Not a blade, not even a heatlance."

Finn shrugged. "What's it matter, if they can be killed other ways?"

"Not much, I s'pose," Baer agreed. "But I'm kinda curious. You know yourself what the spywings're like inside. What if the Slavers're like that too?"

"You mean . . . machines?" Finn asked, remembering the glint of metal inside the spywing that he had brought down.

"Yep. Or partly, anyhow." Baer tugged at his beard thoughtfully. "An' if they are – if they've been *made* somehow, like they make the spywings . . . then who or what made 'em?"

It was, Finn thought, quite a question. But he also thought, shivering slightly despite the warmth of the fire, that it wasn't one he really wanted the answer to.

In the course of the next few days' travel, and the nights of talk, Finn continued to listen and learn. Baer particularly enjoyed telling tales about his adventures since he had escaped from the Slaver centre, and about his continuing one-man war against the aliens. But he was always ready to mix into these tales more of the factual details that Finn hungered for.

"One funny thing 'bout Slavers," he said during one of the evenings, "they got no imagination. They're smart enough, sure – smarter'n people, no question 'bout it. But their heads kinda think in dead straight lines, an' one step at a time. An' that makes 'em wide open to folks like us."

"How?" Finn asked interestedly.

"'Cause they can't be sure what we're gonna do – or why. I've seen it. I've killed me a Slaver, an' gone away. 'Nother Slaver comes along, sees the dead one. He can't figure who or what killed it. He looks 'round awhile, can't find anythin', an' just turns round an' goes home. No imagination." The deep bass chuckle rumbled from the vast chest. "All you gotta do to outthink 'em, no matter how smart they are, is use your imagination. Do things a bit crazy, a bit unexpected, an' they'll have no idea what hit 'em."

So the days of hard travel and the nights of talk went on. And in the process Finn became slowly aware that something odd was happening.

He and Baer were as totally different as two individuals could be. They had come together by accident, and stayed together through an almost casual and, it seemed, temporary agreement. In other circumstances they might have been deadly enemies. Yet somehow, through those days and nights, a bond was developing. Something beyond mere companionship, beyond the brief sharing of the same space. Unlikely as it was, they were becoming friends.

If he had been asked, Finn might have said that there was no place in his life for friendship. The fierce, steely determination that had taken him over when he had first learned of Josh and Jena being taken – and that had been made colder and harder during his grim pursuit – seemed to possess him totally. The bleak numbness that had swept through him, when Baer had revealed what happened to the Slavers' young female captives, still showed in his eyes, and seemed to impose an aloofness on his personality that had not been there before.

Yet at the same time Finn was a young man, who had set out alone into a world he knew little of, to confront an enemy he knew even less of, and carrying as he went a huge burden of pain and sorrow and loss. Without knowing it, he very much needed a friend. And Baer, Bloodkin-born or not, was ideally suited to be that friend.

Their growing closeness became especially clear to Finn, and perhaps to Baer as well, on the fifth night of their travels together. Baer had been reminiscing about his younger days, when Finn had suddenly asked him how he had come by his name, and what it meant.

Baer tugged at his beard and shifted uneasily, trying to change the subject. But Finn, intrigued, pressed him.

"It's a sorta stupid story," Baer mumbled at last. "You'll prob'ly laugh yourself sick."

"I won't laugh," Finn promised.

Baer leaned forward with a small stick, and scratched the four letters on the ground – B A E R. "You read?" he asked, glancing up.

"Some," Finn said. "Josh had a few books from the

73

Forgotten Time, and taught me a bit."

Baer grunted. "Sounds quite a fella, your pa. World needs a few more like him. Now me, I never learned readin'. Bloodkin don't. But sometimes the Slavers dug up old books an' stuff, an' I stole some 'fore the Bloodkin could use 'em to start fires. Learned a few letters, anyways. An' how to write my name."

"What about your name?" Finn persisted.

A gusty sigh. "See, the Bloodkin give names to their little ones. Mostly somethin' to do with the way they look an' act – an' most times not very pretty. Like I knew one called Scarbelly, an' Gaptooth, stuff like that. An' then there was me." Baer scratched ruefully at his beard. "I'm a kinda hairy fella, as you mighta noticed. An' when I was young, I was even more of a yella colour than I am now. The other ones, they used to laugh – till I got my full growth, an' could mash some heads. Anyways, they gave me this name, on account of the yella hair. Only when I got older, I shortened it some – an' ended up bein' Baer."

"But what *was* the name?" Finn demanded.

"If you gotta know," Baer growled, "they called me – Barleyhair."

For a prolonged moment Finn sat staring at Baer with a totally expressionless face. But there was a redness creeping under his skin, and a growing tightness about his mouth, and a strange shaking that he could not control in his body. And at last there was no holding it back. Finn exploded into a howl of laughter.

"*Barleyhair!*" he choked, and laughed until tears streamed from his eyes and his ribs felt as if they were collapsing.

And by then Baer was laughing too, a huge bass booming like a mighty drum. Passing forest creatures paused in the darkness, startled, staring with wonderment at the two people rocking back and forth, clutching their

74

sides, while the wilds echoed with the unfamiliar sound of laughter.

At last the sound subsided, as Finn tried gaspingly to recover, and Baer's great bellows faded to a resonant chuckle. "Son," he said finally, "it'd be a favour to me if you'd put what I told you clean outa your mind."

"I'll have to," Finn said, still sounding half-strangled, "or I'll split myself open."

"Yep, well, laughin's good for what ails you," Baer rumbled. "An' I figure you been needin' some kinda medicine, awhile now."

There was no doubt about that, Finn was musing to himself the following night. The burst of hilarity had seemed to lift a shadow, release a tension, from his inner being. The pain and the loss that he felt were still there, still strong, as was his fierce determination. But they were no longer a crushing burden, threatening to squeeze the very heart and soul from him, to leave him a cold, bitter and empty husk, moving on his quest like a machine. Or like, he thought sourly, an imitation Slaver.

And it had been Baer who had given him that first step to recovering himself, to becoming a human being again. Baer – his friend.

Finn was jogging silently through thick brush, in the early dusk, carrying the limp bodies of three fat quail that would provide that evening's supper. During the day, as during all the days since he had been travelling westwards, they had covered a considerable stretch of wilderness without seeing the faintest sign of other presences, alien or human. But even so Finn's watchful alertness, as much a part of him as his skin, did not slacken.

So he did not miss the flicker of movement, high overhead, half-obscured by the foliage above him.

75

A chill lifted the hair on the back of his neck. Almost without breaking stride, he leaped for a handhold on a tree limb, and was swarming up through the branches with the agility of a squirrel.

Near the top of the tree, his line of sight no longer blocked, he saw with a sinking heart that his first guess, about what he had glimpsed in the sunset-reddened sky, had been correct.

The batshape of a Slaver spywing, flying in a straight unhurried line, towards the north.

Finn watched it steadily, knowing that the tree's abundant leaves would conceal him. But he felt cold fingers grip his heart as he saw the eerie creature's line of flight suddenly change.

It veered to one side, in a sweeping curve that became a descending, circling movement – as a hunting hawk would circle, above its unsuspecting prey.

Finn's intuitive sense of direction confirmed the chill he felt. Below where the spywing was circling, he knew, was a small patch of open grass, on the sun-warmed western side of a low rise.

The place where he had left Baer.

Recklessly he plunged down from branch to branch, and struck the ground running. But even then he knew he was too late.

The spywing had completed its circling survey of the ground beneath it. It had risen higher in the sky again, and had resumed its arrow-straight course towards the north.

10

The Stalkers

WHEN FINN REACHED the patch of open grass, Baer was sitting quietly, enjoying the warmth of the evening, using the heavy machete to peel the bark from a slender green stick.

"Did you see it?" Finn yelled.

Baer gave a huge start, and whirled, nearly dropping the machete.

"Dam', boy," he growled, "wish you'd shuffle your feet or somethin'. Comin' up never makin' a sound, then yellin' like that – I near cut a finger off."

"Did you *see* it?" Finn repeated, urgently.

"See what?" Baer frowned – but the look turned to anxious apology when Finn told him about the spywing.

"Never saw a thing," he said. "Never thought to look. Reckon it saw me, though."

"What do we do?" Finn asked.

Baer shrugged. "Nothin'. Whatever it saw, the Slavers've already seen, wherever they are. Those things, they sorta send pictures back to where they're based. I figure some Slavers'll come out 'fore long, to see what a Bloodkin is doin' out here by himself."

Finn glanced at the western horizon, at the shadows of twilight gathering among the trees around them. "Would they come at night?"

"Yep. Daylight or dark, makes no difference to them."

Finn's teeth flashed in what was not quite a grin. "Then let's wait here for them, and see what happens. How many would come?"

"Maybe one or two." Baer was also grinning, with fierce approval. "Wouldn't think they'd need more, if all they saw was me."

"So we'll surprise them," Finn said.

"That we will," Baer rumbled, hefting the machete. "Just hope they don't come 'fore supper's ready."

In fact the three birds – spitted on the green stick Baer had been peeling, and roasted over a bright bed of coals – had been reduced to gnawed bones, and the deep starlit blackness of full night had gathered, and still no alien sounds had come to disturb the forest quiet.

"If they're comin' at all," Baer growled, hitching closer to the fire, "they must be comin' from a long ways away."

Finn glanced round at the darkness. "Maybe I should go north a way, and scout around."

"That figures," Baer said with his crooked grin. "The spywing just saw *me*, so you're gonna leave me on my own. Like bait."

"You don't have to be," Finn assured him.

Baer chuckled. "Nope, it's good thinkin'. I'm not gonna be much good crashin' around out there in the dark. You go on. But I'd kinda like it if you could stop any of 'em from usin' me for heatlance target practice."

"They won't," Finn promised.

Then he was gone – leaving Baer blinking and shaking his head at the way he had melted into the darkness. "That boy comes an' goes like a puff of smoke," Baer muttered to himself, as he leaned towards the firelight to inspect the gleaming edge of his machete.

Out in the woods, Finn was flitting among the trees more like a shadow than a puff of smoke. He had never looked directly at the fire, so his night vision was intact. Hardly a leaf moved where he passed. A family of rabbits, feeding on a patch of grass, did not even raise their ears, though he went by within a few strides of them. An owl, drifting among the branches, did not change direction or blink an eye, though it flew a tree's width away from Finn. Yet Finn was moving at speed, rapidly widening the distance between himself and Baer.

But after several minutes he came to a sudden halt, seeming almost to become part of the tree trunk that he stood behind. Whatever intuition it was that had prompted him to move into the woods, he was grateful to it.

Because in the distance ahead, barely detectable through the brush, he could hear the sound of something heavy pushing among the trees, and could see faint glimpses of an eerie, spinning, luminescent glow.

A Slaver whirlsled.

Shortly the egg-shaped machine drew near the spot where Finn had paused. It was moving slowly, impeded by the brush, weaving an erratic path among the trees. Yet clearly its driver was keeping the sled on a course that would lead, as directly as possible, to the place where Baer waited alone.

The sled hummed on through the darkness. There was not the remotest chance that its occupant, or occupants, could have noticed the almost invisible shadow that was Finn, drifting among the trees to one side, keeping pace with the alien machine.

As the trees thinned out near the place where Baer sat, the whirlsled picked up speed, sweeping up the low incline in a humming rush, curving to an abrupt halt only a few paces from the fire where Baer was calmly watching its approach.

At once the top of the vehicle was flung open, and two

Slavers emerged. They both had heatlances, but were dangling them almost casually from their clawed hands. They're not a bit worried, Finn thought to himself as he watched from the darkness. Like Baer says – they can't imagine that there could be any danger to them.

The Slavers stepped towards the fire, spatters of their clicking language coming from their lipless mouths. Obviously they were demanding some explanation of Baer's presence. And then Finn was surprised to hear a passable, if deeper-toned, version of the same sounds coming from Baer, as he slowly rose to his feet. Finn was not surprised, though, to see Baer's machete close to hand – standing upright, point-down in the soft turf, as if Baer had just idly jabbed it into the ground.

The Slavers spoke again, gesturing with the heatlances. Baer shrugged, and replied briefly. Finn could not guess what he had said, but the words brought both heatlances sharply up, aiming ominously at Baer's broad chest.

The next word Baer said was spoken quietly, but carryingly – and not in the Slaver tongue.

"Finn?"

"Right here," Finn said. He had already unwrapped his sling, and the heaviest stone he carried rested within it.

At the sound of his voice both Slavers whirled, their yellow eyes shifting at once to a deep crimson. And the heatlances flared, blasting lines of fire through the darkness towards the sound of Finn's voice.

But both rays missed Finn, for he had ghosted to one side as soon as he had spoken. And as he moved, the sling blurred in the air in its whistling spin, and flung the sharp-edged stone crashing into the left eye of the nearest Slaver.

The alien staggered back, a high stuttering howl bursting from its gaping mouth. The second Slaver, eyes darkened now to deep purple, swung its heatlance menacingly, seeking the hidden attacker.

But it did not fire. Baer's machete glinted orange in the firelight, and sliced through the Slaver's neck as though it had been a grassblade.

Finn leaped forward, knife in hand, but by the time he reached the fire the machete had come round again in a backswing, and the second Slaver head, with its crushed eye, rolled gruesomely on the ground.

"Good shot, that," Baer said to Finn, wiping his machete on a handful of grass.

Finn nodded absently, staring down at the decapitated bodies, the green ooze from the severed necks seeming black in the firelight.

Baer sheathed the machete. "We better get movin'. This place'll be crawlin' with Slavers, come mornin'."

Finn looked at him curiously. "Other Slavers will know these two are dead?"

"Yep. Dunno how, but they always seem to know."

"Then other Slavers," Finn said thoughtfully, "will know what happened to that base in the valley."

"Bound to," Baer said. "Leastways, they'll know *somethin'* happened. But they won't figure out what, or how — an' they'd never guess it was a human did it. Unless they find some of those folks you set free, an' get a Bloodkin to make 'em talk."

Finn glanced up, reflexively, at the starbright sky, and Baer followed his glance.

"We got time," he rumbled. "If they were usin' spywings, they'd be here now. We can get ourselves hid 'fore another sled comes." He turned his gaze towards the alien corpses at his feet. "You wanta take a lance along? Me, I never liked 'em much, but you had one before."

Finn nodded, and scooped up one of the heatlances as Baer stepped forward to peer into the empty whirlsled. Then he withdrew, shaking his head.

81

"Only a few Bloodkin get to learn how to work these things," he explained, "an' I wasn't one of 'em. Too bad – it woulda saved a lotta hikin'. An' they didn't even bring any extra charges for the lance."

Finn shrugged, unperturbed.

"I've been thinking," he said. "Maybe we should swing north awhile."

"That figures." Baer grinned. "You wanta back-track this sled, have a look at the Slaver base it came from?"

"We've found nothing else, all this time," Finn pointed out. "I can't just go on without taking a look."

"Suits me," Baer said. "Long's you can find the place without spendin' days sniffin' round."

"I'll find it," Finn promised. "And I'll keep us hidden from spywings and Slavers along the way."

By mid-morning of the next day, Finn and Baer were sprawled full length on damp earth in the depths of a leafy thicket, the heatlance Finn had acquired lying close to hand. Baer had not enjoyed their entrance into the thicket – "all bugs an' thorns", as he saw it – but Finn knew that a Slaver would need almost to step on them to discover them. And the foliage kept them hidden from spywings above, as well.

It was just the hiding place they needed. Two whirlsleds were humming slowly past, heading towards the spot where Baer and Finn had left the remains of the previous night's encounter.

The sleds moved out of sight among the trees, but still Finn and Baer lay where they were, silent and unmoving. Earlier, just before Finn had found the hiding place, he had looked up through the dense trees and had seen a spywing in the distance, flapping in a long, lazy circle through the cloudless sky. The creature kept up its sweeping, searching circle all the while that the two whirl-sleds approached and passed – and still kept it up afterwards.

"If one more of these little critturs bites me," Baer said in a rumbling whisper, "I'm gonna go out an' take my chances with the Slavers."

Finn jabbed him back into silence with an elbow. The insects did not trouble him, nor did the inactivity. If he was going to have a look at the Slaver base to the north, it would be better to do so without two whirlsleds pursuing him. So he kept himself still, waiting with a predator's patience.

By the time that the sun was well past its noon zenith, the whirlsleds appeared again – retracing their path, towards the north. Finn would have given much to know what the Slavers had thought about the corpses they had found – if they thought anything at all. But at least they did not seem inclined to launch an extensive search of the area. For within a few moments the spywing also broke out of its sweeping circle, and soared out of sight northwards.

For half an hour longer, to be safe, Finn insisted on waiting where they were, despite Baer's muttered grumbling. But neither sleds nor spywing reappeared.

"Like I told you," Baer said as they crawled out of the thicket at last. "Slavers got no imagination. Facts're all they know. They couldn't guess what happened – 'cause they don't know how to guess."

Finn had no trouble, this time, picking up the trail. He had three whirlsleds to track, and the last two of them had covered the same route coming and going. Even so, Baer marvelled at the fact that Finn seemed to know where he was going. Several times Finn pointed to signs that shouted aloud to him – branches of a low shrub bent aside, a faint abrasion on the smooth bark of a sapling.

But Baer looked blank. All branches grew in different directions, as far as he could see, and all tree-bark showed odd marks. To Baer, what Finn was doing was little short of magic – especially when he was doing it at the speed of an easy jog-trot, sliding through the undergrowth as if it didn't exist.

But their pace slowed, some hours on. The land had begun to open out, into broad sunlit areas that held only scattered groves of trees, mostly evergreens, and clumps of shrubbery sprouting here and there from the coarse grass. Yet despite the openness, the going was still no easier, for the ground had become rough and uneven, full of humps and hillocks, with many outcroppings of grey rock thrusting up through the thin soil.

Still, as late afternoon approached, the sky remained empty of anything save a few puffs of cloud, and the wilderness remained untroubled by alien machines. And Finn was feeling almost at peace, loping over the sun-warmed grass on the upwards rise of a long, shallow, sweeping incline dotted with crumbling rock and clusters of small firs.

But at the crest of the incline, there was an end to peace.

In the distance, he had glimpsed the sheen of metal, a flash of reflected sunlight through the intervening trees.

Baer caught the same glimpse. Without needing to be told, he dropped as Finn had into a crouch, and wordlessly followed as Finn moved forward into cover. For nearly a kilometre they continued their stealthy advance, Finn gripping the heatlance at the ready, keeping a curtain of evergreens between themselves and the source of the light flash.

At last they crept to the edge of a particularly large stand of firs, and gazed across at the expanse of another, slightly steeper incline, a shallow-sloping and grassy hill.

From its top rose an oddly angled, box-like metal structure, larger than a human house.

"That's the base," Baer grunted.

Finn nodded, studying the building. But then his gaze shifted quickly. From the far side of the hill, behind the structure, a considerable crowd had come into view.

The distance was too great even for Finn's eyes to pick out faces. But he had no trouble seeing that some of the crowd were humans, and some were of the bestial brood that called themselves the Bloodkin. As he watched, other groups straggled over the hill. At a rough count, there were sixty or seventy humans, and at least two dozen Bloodkin.

They were moving – slowly, because as usual the humans were trudging along with the abject weariness of the totally crushed in spirit – towards the alien building. As they neared it, Finn saw the movement of a door sliding open.

"There's a lot of them for such a small place," he said, puzzled.

"That's just the top," Baer said. "Most times, with the bigger centres – an' this one seems pretty big – Slavers build underground. Just the one door, but inside that hill it'll be like an ants' nest."

Finn had other questions, but forgot them when he spotted a flurry of movement at the rear of the main crowd. At once several of the Bloodkin turned and hurried towards it, and the orange-red flare of their forcewhips was unmistakable.

"Somethin's happenin'," Baer growled.

"I'm going closer," Finn decided.

"Finn—" Baer began, warningly.

"They won't see me," Finn said. "Wait for me here – and keep down."

He moved sideways, silent as a falling leaf, and vanished

among the trees. Baer sighed, and turned his attention back to the distant hillside. The flurry of activity was still going on – the crowd of humans milling aimlessly, the flash of forcewhips in the middle of the throng. Baer watched, mystified, trying to guess what was happening – so that it seemed only moments before Finn materialized again at his side, as if rising from the earth itself.

Baer glanced round and concern creased his broad forehead. Finn looked ghastly. He had gone ice-pale beneath his tan, and his hands, clenched into fists so tight that the knuckles were bloodless, were shaking slightly. His lips were drawn back like the snarl of a wolf, and there was a wild light in his eyes that chilled Baer's blood.

"They were beating him," Finn said, his voice strange and harsh. "A man had fallen, and the beasts – the Bloodkin – were hitting him, with their whips, hitting and hitting him. He just lay there, curled up, and they hit him, and laughed. All of them – laughing."

"Easy, now," Baer said gently, reaching out a hand.

"I moved closer," Finn said, as if he had not heard, "and I could see their faces. They were laughing, but they seemed crazy. And the man on the ground was bleeding, and that seemed to make them crazier. They wouldn't stop. They were killing him."

He turned his wild eyes towards Baer. "Then some of the crowd moved a little, and I got a better look at the man on the ground. I saw his face.

"Baer – it was Josh."

PART THREE

The Alien Lair

11

The Tunnel

"I'M GOING IN," Finn said.

He was calmer now, no longer pale, his hands still. But the wildness remained in his eyes, somehow intensified by the bright moon that had risen with the arrival of night. It was a look that made Baer want to shiver, though the night was warm.

They had waited among the trees, watching in grim silence as the humans were herded by the Bloodkin into the metal building. Two of the humans struggled under the weight of a limp human form – the man who had been beaten, the man who was surely Josh Ferral. Baer did not doubt that, for he knew the keenness of Finn's eyes. But he had doubts in plenty about everything else.

"Finn, you can't," Baer said, as he had said several times. "You prob'ly couldn't even open the door. An' if you could, they'd spot you an' kill you inside two paces."

"Maybe not," Finn said stubbornly.

Cursing to himself, Baer tugged at his beard, wishing he could think of something useful to say, wishing this was just another night when they were sitting by a cheery fire feasting on whatever supper Finn had provided. But there was no fire, and no food, this night.

"Dam', boy," Baer growled, "what good'll you be to your pa if you get yourself killed in there?"

"What good am I to him out here?" Finn flared.

"You're alive, that's what," Baer replied. "An' you can still think, an' keep watch, see what's happenin'. Maybe we'll get some luck."

"And maybe in the meantime Josh will die."

"Son," Baer burst out, "you don't know that he isn't dead already, from that whippin'!"

"That's right," Finn snapped. "I don't *know*. Don't know if he's alive, don't know if Jena is in there too. So I'm going in to find out. Now. Tonight." He stood up. "Baer, this is what I came to do. This is why we've been travelling the wilderness all this time. I've got to try. And I'll go alone – no sense both of us taking the risk."

One great hand reached to grip Finn's arm as Baer heaved himself to his feet. "Now, hold on, young Finn. Don't go vanishin' into the dark like you do. You think ol' Baer's gonna let you go an' kill Slavers all by yourself?"

For a moment the ghost of a smile showed at the corners of Finn's mouth. Then he turned silently, with Baer close behind, and moved away into the night.

They travelled in a wide circle, keeping well away from the Slaver base. And they travelled with – for Finn – agonizing slowness and care. Finn knew that, however hard Baer tried, he would probably never be able to move cat-stealthy through the wilds. Yet silence was crucial. For all Finn's impatient urge to blast his way through the building's door with the heatlance, he was still a forest creature. It was instinctive for him to want to examine every centimetre of the terrain before committing himself.

Slowly and cautiously they continued their circle. Every few minutes Finn would leave Baer, warning him to stay still, and disappear into the darkness – so he could creep closer and examine the moonlit building from a new angle. Then he would reappear, and they would move on.

After several of these forays, Baer was feeling relieved

that at least Finn wasn't going to lose his head and go charging crazily in. But then Finn returned, from looking at the back of the Slaver base, with what for Baer was not good news.

"They've been doing some kind of digging," Finn whispered, "on the south side of the hill. I'm going up to look at it."

"I'm comin' too," Baer said at once.

"There's almost no cover," Finn said. "A spywing would spot you for certain. Wait for me here."

"No, Finn—" Baer began. But too late. Where Finn had been crouching was now just a segment of empty night air.

Baer moved tentatively forward, step by slow step, trying to be careful not to rustle the thin grass or step on a twig. Eventually his feet told him that the ground was beginning to rise more steeply. On hands and knees, he crept cautiously forward a few more paces, and peered out from behind a sheltering evergreen.

The gentle, broad slope of the hillside was nearly bare, as Finn had said – only a few small trees, and some narrow patches of deep shadow that were probably low-lying bushes of some sort. Yet there was no sign of Finn. Baer peered till his eyes ached, listened till he felt his ears were stretching like elastic. But the night remained as soundless as the moon itself.

Then – a flicker of movement. It lasted no more than the blink of an eye, so Baer was not fully sure he had seen anything. But it had looked like a human head and shoulders rising briefly out of the grass, halfway up the hill, moonlight gleaming on a thatch of light hair. Somehow Finn had snaked up the bare hillside without so much as disturbing a blade of grass.

For what seemed like hours more, Baer crouched behind the evergreen, grinding his teeth with frustration. As so often before, he almost bellowed aloud with surprise when he felt Finn's touch on his arm.

"I don't think I'm ever gonna get used to this," he grumbled, trying to gather his jangled nerves.

Finn seemed not to have heard him. "They've dug out a good-sized tunnel," he said quickly. "But they've put sheets of metal across the mouth of it."

Baer flexed his enormous shoulders. "Want me to come an' move 'em?"

"No, you'd be seen out there," Finn said. "But there's a way past. Some of the rock at the edge has crumbled a bit – and I might be able to squeeze between it and the metal."

Baer nodded unhappily, seeing what Finn was leading up to. "But it's too tight a squeeze for ol' Baer, right? That figures."

"Don't worry," Finn said. "If the tunnel doesn't lead anywhere, I'll be back."

"An' if it does?"

"If the tunnel leads into the base," Finn said grimly, "I'm going in."

"You want me just to sit here," Baer rumbled, "wonderin' what's happenin' to you?"

"If I'm not back by tomorrow midday," Finn said, "you can reckon I'm not coming."

"An' then," Baer growled, "I might just tear the top off this place an' slice me a few necks." He looked hopefully at Finn. "You sure you couldn't make it by sun-up?"

"Midday," Finn repeated firmly. He closed a fist, and tapped Baer on one great shoulder. "Take care of yourself."

"Finn—" Again Baer found himself talking to an unoccupied piece of darkness. "You too, boy," he said softly. "You too."

*

Again Finn slid up the moon-washed hillside, flat on his belly, the Slaver heatlance thrust through his belt at the back. He seemed to be propelling himself only with fingers and toes, moving forward a few centimetres at a time, finding natural channels among the tufts of thin grass. No abnormal movement of the grass betrayed his presence, and in the deceptive light and shadow created by the moon even a spywing would have had to be hovering low, directly above, to spot him.

But if there were spywings aloft on night patrol, they were not looking at the south side of the hill. He reached the mouth of the tunnel without incident. As he had told Baer, it was a recently dug opening, wearing a temporary cover of heavy sheet metal, fixed to the rocky edges.

Finn snaked round the cover towards the spot he had located before. Also as before, he had to lift his head and shoulders a little, to tug at fragments of the crumbling rock that made a narrow gap at one side of the metal cover. The rock crumbled further, widening the gap, until the opening was large enough. Headfirst, wary and slow, with the heatlance now ready in his hand, Finn wriggled through.

On the other side of the opening, the shaft of the tunnel angled down at an easy slope, into the depths of the hillside. It was wide enough for two men to stand abreast, but low enough to force them into a crouch. The moon's ghostly light filtered in through Finn's place of entry, so that his night vision could see the dirt walls and dusty floor of the tunnel. And he could also see the different floor at the far end of the tunnel – a flat, hard surface of metal.

Deep within the hillside, the tunnel had opened into a high-ceilinged, metal-walled, artificial cavern – a vault.

The moonlight was dimmer there, but it was still enough for Finn to see the shapes of large metal boxes and cases, some almost as tall as himself, stacked around the walls of the vault, leaving a clear area in the centre. Though Finn had no experience of such things, he felt certain that the vault was no part of the Slaver base. It had to be a human construction – a leftover from the Forgotten Time.

The Slavers might have found the vault by accident, he thought, while they were building their base. Or they might have built the base here because they were drawn to the spot by the presence of the vault. Finn would never know which – but in any case it mattered little to him.

What did matter was that the vault appeared to be a dead end.

Silently he moved round the vault, peering at the cases, squeezing behind them to examine the metal walls, by touch more than sight. The cases themselves were mysteries, even when a stray moonbeam slanted in from the tunnel mouth and spotlighted a printed word, faintly visible on the outside of one case – USAF.

It was not a word that held meaning for Finn. Nor did the contents of one of the cases, whose lid he found loosened by corrosion. Long, heavy, cylindrical objects of dark metal, with other odd words printed on them. What, he wondered idly, had 'Thermal Grenade Launcher' meant to the men of the distant past?

But it was no time to ponder ancient mysteries. His survey of the vault had shown only that the passage of time had done it little good. The metal of the walls, like the cases, had suffered corrosion and weakening. There were many cracks spiderwebbing the metal, and the ceiling looked far from secure.

Finn stood still, thinking hard. The tunnel came in from the south, so he knew which direction the Slaver base would lie, in relation to the vault. And, knowing the length of the tunnel and the breadth of the vault, he believed that the two underground structures could not be too far apart.

He moved to the wall that, by his reckoning, should lie next to the Slaver base. Near the floor it offered just what he wanted – a narrow split in the weakened metal. He slid his knife-blade into the crack, expecting to feel the solidity of earth and rock beyond it. But the blade went through unimpeded, into empty air.

Carefully, Finn thrust the slim tube of the heatlance into the crack at its widest point. And when the lance had reached in almost to its full length, the tip struck against a barrier – with the faint but unmistakable *clank* of metal on metal.

Finn jerked the lance back. It had to be the outer wall of the Slavers' underground base that he had touched. But had the faint noise alerted anyone – or any*thing* – within the base?

For a moment he considered fleeing from the vault. He had no wish to be trapped there by a horde of armed Bloodkin, coming round to attack him from the tunnel.

But instead he settled for creeping to the tunnel mouth and crouching there, listening. For many moments he waited, motionless. His acute hearing would have picked up the sound of a mouse breathing in the grass on the slope outside. But he heard no sound of approaching Bloodkin. The night was as silent as before.

It was also well advanced, he realized, noting the angle of the moonlight. If he still hoped somehow to enter the Slavers' base during the hours of darkness, he saw that he needed to hurry. There were too few of those hours left.

But that meant that he had to decide between two courses of action. He either had to take a risk that was almost inconceivable. Or he had to do something else that was even more inconceivable – leave the vault and the tunnel, admit defeat, turn his back on Josh.

There was, after all, no choice.

He crept back to the far wall of the vault where the narrow crack awaited him. Staring at it for a moment, he felt icy sweat burst out on his skin, and fought to control a faint tremor in his hands. If he could have thought of any other way to gain entry to the alien base, he would have grasped it with desperate relief. But there was no other way.

The wild light flared again in his eyes as he raised the heatlance – and directed its blazing, irresistible ray at the crack in the wall of the vault.

12

Underground Search

THE FURIOUS RAY made short work of the vault's corroded metal wall. In moments Finn had carved a gap large enough for him to squeeze through. But beyond the gap was half a metre of empty space and total inky darkness. And beyond that space . . .

For a second his hands stiffened, as if they had minds of their own and were resisting what he was about to do. But he forced them to move, to raise the heatlance again.

. It was an insane risk. He had not the slightest idea what lay beyond the wall of the Slaver base – what kind of alien horror might be waiting for him, alerted by the unavoidable sound of his entry. Yet there was no going back.

Again the crimson ray flashed out, biting now into the smooth metal wall of the Slaver base.

Molten metal sizzled and sputtered, and to Finn each burst of noise seemed like sky-shattering thunder. At any moment he expected to hear the tunnel behind him echoing with the monstrous fury of the Bloodkin. Or were the Slavers holding them back, waiting for him to cut his way through the metal, to leap upon him then inside the base?

These possibilities and worse swarmed through Finn's imagination like demonic visions. But still the powerful ray chewed steadily at the alien metal, and the gap in the Slavers' wall opened more widely.

Finally it was large enough to admit his body. Not daring to hesitate in case he froze completely, Finn flung himself across the narrow space between the vault and the base – and entered the lair of the Slavers.

And there was no sound of movement, not the faintest hint of danger, in the place where he found himself.

It was a smallish chamber, its metal walls weirdly angled, forming too many corners. A dim glow seemed to emanate from the walls themselves, enough to allow Finn to see clearly. He saw what was some kind of foodstore, no doubt for the provisions that fed the Bloodkin – for among the foodstuffs were great chunks of meat, piled on one side and stinking foully. But Finn's keen sense of smell told him that the evil stench of the place was also partly made up of the rank odour of the Bloodkin themselves – and, faint but detectable, the smell of stale human sweat, and the reek of human fear.

Some of that fear, Finn thought, was certainly his own. Yet despite the fact that his limbs felt as if they were being bathed in icy water, he crept forward. There was a section of the far wall that looked like it might be a door – and so it proved, for as he neared it, it slid silently open, like the iris of an eye.

The door was half-way along a short, broad corridor, which also had dimly glowing metal walls, and was entirely bare and silent. The corridor was not straight, though bent in the Slaver manner that ignored right angles, and Finn could see two more of the iris-doors, one at each end. He moved cautiously ahead, step by nerve-wracked step.

And still there was no sound of activity, or alarm. Somehow the noise of his forced entry – which would not truly have been as noisy as it had seemed to Finn – had been muffled and contained within the closed storeroom. The base remained silent, undisturbed.

And Finn moved through it, soundless as a feather, his boots hardly seeming to touch the floor.

Some time later – Finn had no idea how long, though it seemed like centuries – he had a clearer idea of the shape of the underground structure. And Baer had been right, when he compared it to an ants' nest.

Each of the misshapen, many-cornered chambers led to more chambers, either through interconnecting doors or along more of the short, bare corridors. There were at least several dozen of the chambers behind Finn now – though he had kept fixed in his mind a general idea of their layout, trusting his sense of direction to lead him back to the gap in the storeroom wall.

That directional sense also told him more or less how far underground he was. So he realized that the base must have another level, above the one he had entered. But he had no idea how it could be reached. He had seen no stairways, ladders or other ways of moving between levels.

In some of the corridors, he had seen odd vertical shafts of glowing light that shone down from not-quite-circular openings in the metal ceiling. The openings were large enough for him to climb through, if he could reach them. But he had not tried. The glowing light was yellowish, not red, yet it reminded him of the sparkling luminescence beneath a whirlsled. And he had no wish to find out how it might affect human flesh.

In any case, there was still more of the lower level to investigate. As far as he could tell, he had been moving through chambers round the outer area of the base. They had offered little of interest or information. More storerooms, some filled with mysterious alien machines or parts of machines; others that seemed to be workplaces of some kind, equally mysterious to Finn. He had never seen even a human laboratory, or technological establishment – and he certainly had no way of understanding the purpose of the alien science that he saw.

More important to Finn, in his search of the outer chambers he had not seen a single living thing. Nor had there been even a hint that the occupants of the base were aware of an intruder, or that they were lurking somewhere to attack him.

But by the time he had ventured into some of the other chambers, he was almost wishing that they would.

What he saw drove all fear from his being, and left him trembling with a hate-filled rage that threatened to send him berserk.

One of the inner chambers was another storeroom. But this time there was no mystery about what was stored there. Large transparent containers, standing all around the walls, held portions of human bodies. Heads, hands, arms, internal organs – all floating in some preservative liquid, like exhibits in the ghastly museum of a mass murderer.

And if that chamber left Finn shaken, one farther on nearly made him weep. It was crammed with low, hard pallets that made crude and uncomfortable beds. And these were occupied by young human women – more than a dozen of them, alive, but dirty and ragged and painfully thin. A few of the women had the swollen abdomens of the later stages of pregnancy. Others were clutching tiny, sleeping infants.

Infants that were heavy-limbed, sharp-toothed, and covered with a thick down of tangled fur.

Fighting his rage and nausea, Finn moved quietly into the room. But a few of the women were awake – and the sight of Finn sent them shrinking away, like the captives in the valley, eyes wide and glazed with terror.

Finn paused, looking around, guiltily aware that mingled with his anger and horror was a feeling of relief. None of these women was his foster sister.

He leaned close to one of the women. "Do you know a girl named Jena?" he whispered. "Jena Ferral? Is she here?"

But the woman, no more than a girl herself, pressed back against the wall as far from Finn as she could get, a low moan of fear escaping from her trembling mouth.

Finn backed away quickly. The last thing he wanted was for one of these tormented creatures to scream. In the depths of their suffering they could no longer tell friend from enemy. Every moment of their lives now held horror, pain and despair – and Finn had no time to prove to them that his presence would not merely bring them more.

He slipped out of the room, fighting to restrain the towering fury that was close to driving him mad. In those moments his watchfulness slipped a little – and he had nearly walked straight into the iris-door at the end of another of the short corridors before he realized that, unlike the others, it had not opened at his approach.

He halted, wariness returning. There was another oddness about this door. It glowed faintly, as did all the metal that lined the interior of the base, providing a built-in light source. But this door also seemed to sparkle, with small flecks of crimson dancing in the air directly in front of the iris-opening.

Again Finn was reminded of the cushion of force that the whirlsleds rode on. Instinctively he drew back, his eyes sweeping over the wall on either side of the door. On one side, interrupting the smooth surface, he saw a small near-square of raised metal, with an oddly shaped depression in its centre. It vaguely reminded Finn of the groove on the heatlance, which he still clutched, that fired the weapon.

Nervously, he reached the end of the heatlance forward and lightly touched the depression on the metal square. The crimson glow across the door winked out. And the door slid open.

Finn stared through, into a large, cavernous, stinking chamber. It was crammed with humans – men, sixty or seventy of them, sprawled or curled on the hard floor in the depths of sleep.

But not quite all of them. The door's movement had brought one of the men sitting up in a quick, defensive lunge. He was tall, broad-shouldered, with a scar like a ravine crossing his face from brow to jaw. And both his mouth and his eyes were gaping to their widest extent, with shock.

"Now blast me," the man said hoarsely, "if this ain't one rip-roarer of a dream."

Finn did not hear him, was not looking at him. Others among the men had begun to lift their heads, in startled or terrified wonderment, at the sight of an armed and free human standing in the doorway. And one of those heads was grizzled, with a lined and leathery face, smeared with dried blood from many crusted cuts that showed like stripes across the face and the thin, half-naked body.

"Josh," Finn whispered, barely audible.

The old man seemed terribly weak, barely able to lift his head, because of the fearsome wounds left by the force-whips. But a smile crept across his lined face, and his eyes, as bright as ever, shone with an expression that was both astonishment and unutterable joy, as he looked across the room at Finn.

Finn moved swiftly into the chamber, and the scar-faced man scrambled to his feet. "Fella," the hoarse voice said, "if this's a dream, it's hellish cruel."

"No dream," Finn said brusquely. "I've come for Josh."

"Then you'd be Finn," the man said. "Ol' Josh's been braggin' some 'bout y'. Only seems what he said is the clear truth."

But Finn, brushing past him, had knelt beside Josh. The old man lay on a thin heap of rags, obviously taken from the backs of the other men in a pathetic attempt to ease his pain. Josh reached out a tremulous hand, gripping Finn's wrist.

"Son . . ." His voice was a faint whisper. "Knew you'd come after us. Dam' crazy fool . . ."

"Is Jena here?" Finn asked urgently.

"Nope." The old eyes clouded. "We was . . . separated. Took her in 'nother sled. She's gone, boy."

Though the pain of the words stabbed into Finn like a spear, he tried to keep his voice low and calm. "What about you, Josh? Can you move?"

A ghost of a grim smile creased the old face. "I c'n try. If it kills me . . . I'd a sight rather die somewhere else than here."

"What you plannin'?" The scar-faced man had come over to them. "How y' gonna get Josh out? An' how in hell did y' get *in*?"

By this time all the men were awake, watching Finn with a mixture of fear, disbelief and wild hope in their eyes.

Finn glanced at the scarred man briefly. "No time for talk. Slavers and Bloodkin could be all over us, any minute."

"Not yet," said the scarred man, surprisingly. "Slavers an' them beasts stay up top till daylight. Bloodkin, they like their sleep – 'cept maybe for a guard they put on the outside door up there. An' Slavers, they don't worry none

'bout us, not when we're tucked up behind the heatdoor."
He grinned hugely. "So we got time f'r the whole bunch
of us t' get out."

Finn stared at him. It all seemed so easy. But, as Baer
would say, he thought, it figures. Slavers and Bloodkin
would never think that any human would try to enter a
base – and so would have no reason to be watchful. That
sense of security, and superiority, and the lack of imagination that Baer had described, left the Slavers wide open.

He smiled fiercely at the scarred man. "All right, we'll
go. But quick, and quiet." He swiftly told the man about
the entrance he had cut, in the wall next to the vault.

The man's eyebrows climbed high. "Dam', but y' got
guts. Just show us the way. But listen – we been diggin'
that tunnel an' we know that vault. Whole thing c'd come
down, any time."

Finn shrugged. "It's the only way to go."

"Death's the way we're goin'," muttered a man in the
crowd, and several other voices murmured low agreement.
But they fell silent when the scarred man wheeled and
glared at them.

"Anybody who'd as soon stay an' die here c'n suit
hisself," he snarled. "Anybody who's comin', y' stay shut
tight an' do what this young fella says – or I'll be snappin'
some necks 'fore the night's out."

He turned back from the cowed group of men. "Name's
Gratton," he said to Finn. "You tell us what t' do, we'll
do it." The broad grin flashed again. "Dam' me, young
fella, but bein' free is gonna taste sweet. There'll be a debt
owed t' you we won't know how t' pay."

"We're not out yet," Finn said sharply. "Give me a
hand with Josh."

Swiftly but carefully the two of them lifted the old man.
Josh's legs were shaky, and he was visibly struggling not
to groan aloud with pain as he was moved. Finn braced

103

himself to take most of Josh's weight, and turned towards the door.

Then a thought struck him – and he held the heatlance out to Gratton. "Take this, and keep an eye out behind us. If we get trouble, you can start paying some of that debt."

Pure delight swept over Gratton's scarred face as he grasped the weapon. "Almost hope a few of them beasts come down."

"They will," Finn said, "if we don't get going. It'll be sun-up soon enough."

He moved towards the door, half-carrying the weak and stumbling Josh. Behind him, most of the men followed along, eyes ablaze now with fierce elation. A few remained, huddled into a corner, sweating with terror, and Gratton paused in front of them, glowering. Then he merely spat contemptuously, and followed the others out of the chamber.

Finn was concentrating on his rough mental map of the route he had taken. As yet he could hardly let himself believe what had happened – how easy it had been to penetrate the base, find Josh, and begin an unopposed escape. All he had to do now was to get back to that gap in the wall, as quickly and silently as he could with fifty men trailing behind him.

But they had no sooner stepped out into the corridor when the time of silence ended.

On the upper level, but so loud that it seemed only a few metres away, there erupted an enormous storm of terrifying noise. The ringing of metal on metal – the heavy thudding of running feet – and, rising above it all, the savage bestial roar of an enraged Bloodkin.

13

Discovery

WHILE FINN HAD been prowling the Slaver base, Baer had dutifully remained crouched in the darkness among the evergreens at the foot of the slope where the base stood. It had not been easy, for waiting and hiding did not come naturally to Baer. The night seemed filled with unsettling sounds – the creak of a bough, the almost inaudible rustle of some small creature in the grass. And even more unsettling were the images that filled Baer's mind, of what might be happening to Finn inside the alien base.

Many times he half-rose, feeling that what he should really be doing was following Finn and looking after him, rather than sitting safely under a tree. But each time he sank back into his waiting crouch, remembering with a silent growl that his bulk would not allow him to take the route Finn had taken.

So he waited, nerves fraying with anxiety. And by the time dawn spread a pink glow on the eastern sky, his patience – thin enough at the best of times – had worn away to vanishing point.

He made up his mind. He would go for a brief look around. If Finn returned while he was gone, they would surely be able to find each other. And if Finn didn't return, then there was surely no point in Baer skulking among the trees – which in any case were going to be less safe as a hiding place now that daylight was coming.

As quietly as he knew how, Baer began a cautious circle around towards the front of the Slaver base.

He had no way of knowing that, at the same moment, Finn was stepping into a broad chamber crowded with sixty or seventy startled men.

Nor could Baer know that, just inside the main door to the base, at the top of the hill, a Bloodkin was yawning and stretching his way to full wakefulness.

The Bloodkin had been sleeping by the door, as one of his kind usually did, just in case some technical malfunction might let some of the braver human slaves try to creep away. Something had disturbed this Bloodkin's sleep, but he began to think it was just an early-morning dream, for all was quiet inside the base. So he yawned, and stretched, and scratched his hairy belly, and wished he was asleep again.

But then he rose and touched the mechanism that slid the outer door silently open, intending to get a breath of fresh air. He was a huge, powerful creature with vast sloping shoulders and an equally sloping forehead that indicated a limited intelligence. It was only idleness that sent him shambling out of the base, to stand blinking vacantly in the first light of dawn.

At the edge of the trees below the hill, Baer saw him emerge, and tried to duck back into cover. He moved quickly, but not quite quickly enough. The Bloodkin at the door of the base spotted the movement.

Even then, the Bloodkin's dim brain registered no alarm. The thought that there might be an enemy at the bottom of the slope did not occur to him. There were no enemies. There were the Masters, who frightened and overawed him. And then there were only other Bloodkin, and the human worms – and this giant had never been frightened or alarmed by any of those in his life.

The movement in the trees had to be some kind of wild animal. Out of nothing more than vague curiosity, the giant Bloodkin began to lumber down the hill.

Baer watched him come unhappily. Finn was not going to be pleased that he had moved and had been seen. Yet Baer knew that he lacked the skill simply to slip away into the woods and evade the huge Bloodkin. He also knew that if the giant saw him clearly, it wouldn't do anyone any good – least of all Finn.

Still . . . whatever was to happen would happen.

As the huge Bloodkin drew near, Baer stepped out from among the trees. He, too, was merely sauntering, apparently not looking at the giant. Then he turned his head casually and stopped short, looking surprised.

So did the giant, who *was* surprised. "Hoy!" The shout was thick and guttural. "Who you? How you get out here?"

Appearing wholly untroubled, Baer ambled forward. "How do. Name's Baer. Remember? Came in last week, from over east. An' you're . . ."

"Gash," said the giant, responding automatically. A look of slow puzzlement was creeping over his low, furrowed brow. "Don' 'member you. Las' week?"

"Sure," said Baer, still moving forward. They were near enough now to see each other's faces clearly in the grey light. "You remember, Gash. One of you boys gave me this, when I got here."

'This' was the machete, to which Baer's hand had casually, unhurriedly moved. He had taken a firm grip on the hilt before the puzzlement on Gash's face had begun to change into something like alarm.

But by then it was too late – for alarm, or for the force-whip in Gash's hand. The machete drove hilt-deep into the prominent bulge of the giant's belly, angled upwards to strike the heart.

The huge creature crumpled, his blood crimsoning the grass. Baer stepped round the corpse, bending to wipe his reddened blade on the thick fur of Gash's chest. "Never saw a fella," he said pleasantly, gazing at the gaping wound his machete had made, "with a name that suited him more."

He turned away, glancing up the hill. The outer door of the base still stood open. Invitingly open. It seemed a shame, Baer thought, to pass up such an invitation. Especially when it gave him a way to get where Finn was – just in case he was needed.

Machete in hand and a happy smile on his face, Baer went up the hill in a rush.

Inside the door, he halted. The corridor ahead of him, with its faintly glowing walls, was deserted. But somewhere nearby, he knew, the other Bloodkin would be stirring awake. And also nearby, the Slavers of the base would soon emerge – from whatever they did during the hours of darkness.

Baer hoped desperately that Finn was already out of the base. But he knew that he would have to go down to the lower level and be sure. And there was very little time, if he intended to make his way back again, to leave by the outer door.

Trying to keep his boots quiet on the metal floor, he moved swiftly along the corridor.

And his time ran out. Behind him and ahead of him, doors slid open.

At his back, a Slaver stepped out into the corridor. It seemed to look past Baer, and its eyes remained their normal yellow. Clearly it felt no surprise at seeing a Bloodkin – and clearly it also did not recognize Baer as a stranger.

But ahead of Baer, through the other door that had opened, two Bloodkin lumbered out into the corridor.

108

Less stupid than Gash, they took in at a glance the fact that they did not know Baer, that he carried a naked machete but no forcewhip, and that behind him the outer door to the base stood open.

They growled, like the beasts they were. One raised his whip threateningly – the other reached for the heavy, long-bladed knife at his belt.

Baer did not hesitate. Raising the glittering machete, he launched himself towards them, roaring a ferocious battle cry.

That was the eruption of chilling noise that was heard by Finn and the other men, as they left their sleeping chamber on the level below. Many of the men turned pale and seemed about to panic. But Gratton was behind them, eyes blazing, driving them on.

"Go on, Finn!" he hissed. "Get us out, while the gettin's good!"

And Finn, still supporting the burden of Josh, moved grimly forward into the corridor beyond the chamber, with the others crowding fearfully at his heels.

On the level above, Baer was in full flight. The two Bloodkin had gone down before his furious charge, though not before one had slashed him with the forcewhip and laid a livid weal of pain across his side. And the Slaver behind him had fired its heatlance – but Baer had been lucky, and the lethal ray had only singed the hair on his upper left arm.

By then, he had reached the iris-door at the end of the corridor and flung himself through it. It led into a narrow chamber lined with the eerily motionless batshapes of spy-wings. The creatures were obviously not activated, yet their bulging eyes seemed to follow Baer as he hurtled across the narrow space.

He knew this moment of respite would be brief. He could hear the muffled roaring of Bloodkin all around –

some massing in the corridor he had just left, others rushing through adjoining chambers.

Finn's gonna be mad, he thought sourly, as he leaped through the far door of the chamber.

He heard the angry hiss of the forcewhip before he saw it, yet he was able to block the downward slash, with the machete. The razor edge bit deep into a hairy forearm, and the whip-wielder's growl became a shriek of pain as the blood gouted. But Baer had already rushed past — towards a near-circle of yellow light ahead, in the floor of the corridor.

Without pause, he stepped through the opening, into the shaft of light. He knew about the Slavers' near-magical uses of the energies they controlled, for he had ridden these strange elevators many a time in his youth. His body was grasped in a light, firm, invisible embrace of power — and he was wafted down the shaft to the lower level as if he had wings.

He stepped out of the shaft, into another corridor, in time to see four Bloodkin and a Slaver burst through a door at the far end, in a furious charge.

In another part of the lower level, Finn too was hard pressed. He and the men had made very little progress before they found their way barred. Other Bloodkin, who had rushed down to find Baer, found instead a crowd of escaping slaves. Bellowing with rage, they raised their forcewhips and attacked.

Most of the men fell back in panicky disarray, Finn with them. He heard Gratton's angry shout, and the blaze of the heatlance — but he knew he could not remain to fight. His first concern had to be for Josh. As fear lent strength to the old man's legs, the two of them fled back the way they had come — and plunged through the first door that offered itself.

It was the door into the room where the women were

kept. Even more terrified than before, the women huddled by the far wall, but this time Finn paid them little attention. Another door led out of the room, and into a chamber that Finn had not seen before.

But at least it was not occupied. Just another collection of weird alien machinery, including some delicate-looking implements suspended over a broad, metal table that bore some unpleasant stains. But Finn ignored that. Josh seemed only half-conscious, near to collapse from the pain of the exertion, and Finn knew that the old man would have to rest a moment – whatever the risk – before resuming the escape.

Carefully he lowered Josh on to the table, wondering as he did so how many of the other men had survived that Bloodkin charge, and how many had fled in panic to wander the mazy corridors until they were found by more Bloodkin. At least he knew that Gratton would stand and fight – and maybe others would as well. Something within Finn, born of his rage and hatred, wished that he were standing with them.

But then the fight came to Finn.

The door through which he and Josh had entered slid open. A Bloodkin stood there, snarling horribly, forcewhip flaring.

The monster lunged forward. And Finn, like a wild creature protecting its den, sprang to meet the charge. The forcewhip crackled over his head as he dodged beneath it – and then his hunting knife was in his hand, and its blade was plunging deep into the Bloodkin's chest.

The creature screamed and staggered backwards. Behind it the door slid open again, and the dying Bloodkin stumbled through, Finn's knife still jutting from its chest. Before Finn could reach it, the door had slid shut once more.

Finn drew back into the chamber, preferring to lose the

knife rather than risk leaving the chamber where Josh lay. A swift glance showed him that the old man seemed to have fainted, so that he lay as if sleeping peacefully on the stained table. Finn glanced round the chamber, searching both for another doorway and for something that might serve as a weapon, now that he no longer had heatlance or knife.

But it was neither a door nor a weapon that caught his eye, and stopped him still as if he were encased in ice.

It was the sight, in a far corner, of three large, transparent containers like those that had held the segments of human bodies. But these containers held entire bodies. Very small, and very dead.

Floating in the preservative fluid of each container lay the tiny, wrinkled form of a newborn human baby.

Finn could see that these were not infant Bloodkin, but normal babies. And he could see something else, which was the main cause of the shock that had almost stopped his breath and heart.

Each of the small bare bodies had a strange marking on its upper left arm. Strange . . . but familiar.

An oddly patterned arrangement of raised, dark dots.

Unconsciously Finn's right hand moved up, to brush the fingertips over the pattern of dots on his own arm. Otherwise he did not move. Time seemed to have stopped, as he stood there rooted, paralysed.

His mind was struggling to reject what he was seeing – to avoid realizing what it might mean. Locked in that struggle, he scarcely noticed when a half-hidden inner door, opposite the door he and Josh had come through, slid open.

Nor did he notice the figure standing in the doorway. A tall, spindly figure, with faceted eyes blazing orange-red as fire, and a heatlance clutched in its three-clawed hands.

112

14

Vault of Death

BAER HAD TAKEN one look at the murderous horde charging towards him, as he had stepped from the elevator's shaft of light, and had leaped for the safety of the nearest doorway. Beyond it, he had continued in a headlong rampaging flight that took him through chamber after chamber, corridor after corridor. Once or twice the places he had entered had been occupied, but by Bloodkin who had not been prepared to meet one of their own kind bellowing like a beast run amok, and swinging a bloodstained machete. So a trail of slashed and gory corpses marked Baer's passage through the labyrinth of the lower level.

But the result of that headlong rush was that Baer found himself lost. And soon he came to a halt in the middle of an unoccupied chamber – one of the Slavers' ugly laboratories – to take stock.

As he did so, a familiar sound came to his ears. Not clearly, for it was muffled by intervening doorways, but near enough to be recognizable. The sounds of battle.

Taking a firmer grip on the machete, he headed out of the room, in the general direction of the furore. But as the iris-door parted, he stopped in his tracks, appalled at what he saw.

Another Slaver laboratory. An old man, seeming asleep

or dead, on a bare table. And Finn, slumped on the floor, a stripe of bright blood across his chest, with a Slaver bending over him, grasping at him with its evil claws.

As the Slaver had come through the door, the instincts of a wild creature had awakened within the fog that clouded Finn's brain. He flung himself aside just as the crimson ray leaped from the alien's heatlance. The movement saved his life but did not save him from being grazed by the ray, a slicing blaze across his ribs. He stumbled and fell, the odour of his own burned flesh in his nostrils.

Numbed by the shock of the wound, and perhaps still by the unbelievable horror he had seen before the Slaver entered, Finn felt no pain. His vision seemed unnaturally clear, as he lay bleeding on the metal floor, watching the Slaver move towards him. It appeared to be happening in slow motion – the alien's spindly strides, the lifting of the heatlance that would erase Finn's life. He watched, paralysed, as a bird watches a snake gliding towards it for the kill.

But the Slaver halted. The red blaze of its eyes shifted, to purple and then to a cold and lambent blue. The heatlance swung away, and the alien reached down a clawed hand and grasped Finn's left wrist, twisting his arm round.

It was looking at the marks on Finn's arm.

The Slaver turned its head, and a stream of the rasping, clicking sounds burst from its mouth – as if it were calling to others in an adjoining chamber. But there was no reply – and so the creature turned back to Finn, jerking sharply at his arm as if trying to drag him to his feet.

Finn resisted weakly, but there seemed to be no strength left in his body. Yet the Slaver was unable, by itself, to pull him upright. For a second the strange tug-of-war continued, in a motionless deadlock. Then the Slaver dropped Finn's arm and raised the heatlance menacingly. But if it had intended to fire, it had no chance to do so.

Finn saw something bright and metallic fly over his head, spinning almost lazily, to sink its razor edge deep into the scrawny throat of the Slaver.

A machete. With Baer plunging furiously into the room behind it.

Snatching up his weapon, Baer bent over Finn and grunted with relief that the ray had merely seared flesh and skin.

"We'll get somethin' on that to stop the bleedin'," he growled. "Can you get up?"

But Finn barely saw him. His eyes still held a dazed, faraway expression, seeming to stare at some distant, unknowable horror.

"Finn, c'mon!" Baer said urgently. "They're all around us − we gotta move!"

Finn stirred slightly, as if some part of him was trying to respond. But still his dazed eyes were fixed on something across the room. Baer wheeled, warily − and saw the three tiny, pathetic bodies floating in their transparent containers.

For a moment he stared − and then he realized what had happened. He turned back to Finn, and saw that the dazed stare had shifted. Finn's eyes were now fixed on Baer's own left arm − where the blast from the Slaver heatlance had singed away the thick hair, to reveal another of the strange patterns of raised dark dots.

In one movement, Baer grasped Finn's jerkin, dragged him effortlessly to his feet, and swung one hand in a fierce, open-palmed blow that spun Finn's head halfway round.

The blow broke through the mixture of horror, shock and pain that had been clouding Finn's mind. Awareness leaped back into his eyes and with it an agony that had nothing to do with the wound on his side, or the slap.

"Baer . . ." Finn choked. "The markings . . ."

"No time, boy!" Baer barked. "We gotta get out!"

Unsteadily, Finn began to move towards the three grisly containers. "But what . . ." he began.

"The marks mean nothin', Finn!" Baer raged. "Hear me? *Nothin'!*" A great hand swept up the dead Slaver's heatlance and thrust it roughly at Finn. "Take this, an' get on out! An' *watch* yourself!"

"Josh . . ." Finn said weakly.

"I'll bring the ol' fella! Now *go on!*"

Driven by the desperation in Baer's voice, Finn moved to the door, while Baer scooped up the unconscious form of Josh as if he were a bag of feathers, and hurried after him.

It was the door that led back into the chamber where the women had been kept, but Finn was vaguely surprised to find it deserted. Beyond that room, in the corridor, there were also no living beings – but it was not empty. The floor was stickily awash with blood, and occupied by the scattered corpses of nearly a dozen Bloodkin, and at least twice as many men.

"If there's any humans left alive," Baer rumbled from behind Finn, "they musta scattered. Maybe we can pick some of 'em up – if you can find the way outa here."

The sight of the carnage in the corridor, and the need to escape, seemed to galvanize Finn. He glanced around, trying to gather his scattered thoughts and recall his route through the maze of the lower level. Faintly, he could hear a fearsome chorus of snarling roars, which told him that Bloodkin were gathering somewhere nearby. And that sound galvanized him further. Swiftly he and Baer moved towards the doorway at the far end of the corridor.

Chamber after chamber, corridor after corridor, they

rushed through the maze of the lower level and met no opposition. The sounds of the Bloodkin force behind them grew fainter as they hurried on. But then, as they entered a room that Finn recognized as being near the exit point he was seeking, they found their way barred.

But not by Bloodkin. The room was crowded with wild-eyed, desperate men, most of them bleeding from slashes and burns, all of them armed with weapons taken from dead Bloodkin. There were more than two dozen of them, Finn saw. And among them were the women. Those with infants were still clutching the small furred forms – but most were also clutching Bloodkin weapons, and looking as wild and dangerous as the men.

And at their head was the tall form of Gratton, bearing a few more scars now, but still gripping the heatlance. The big man whirled, startled, as Finn burst into the room – then his eyes changed, and his lance swung up, aiming past Finn's shoulder. At Baer.

"No!" Finn shouted, and sprang forward, swinging his own heatlance. The two weapons clashed ringingly, and Gratton's lance was swept aside, its ray gouging a molten hole in the chamber's wall.

"He's a friend!" Finn yelled. "That's Josh he's carrying!"

Gratton lowered the lance wonderingly. "If you say so, Finn . . ."

"If you're that eager for killin'," Baer's bass rumble broke in, "you're gonna have all you can handle in a minute."

His meaning was clear. During the pause the massed force of Bloodkin had grown nearer. The chilling chorus of yells and growls was no more than a room or two away.

Several of the men began to shout at once, with a variety of suggestions, but Finn's voice cut through the sound impatiently. "Baer, take Josh and keep going. Angle to your left, and look for a food storeroom with a hole in the wall. We'll be right behind you."

Baer nodded and moved towards the far door of the room, the humans drawing nervously back to clear a path for him.

"You people," Finn went on, "follow him, and keep together. Gratton and I will stay back a little, and slow the Bloodkin down."

The group milled about for a moment, anxiously, then crowded out of the door in Baer's wake. Gratton watched them go, pity and anger mingling in his expression.

"Not many left," he said to Finn. "But I'm glad we c'd get the women. They had the worst of it, in this place."

"Then let's get them *out*!" Finn snapped.

Cautiously he moved back towards the door where he and Baer had entered the chamber. It opened on to one of the short corridors – and at the other end, another door was opening, revealing the hulking, jostling forms of many Bloodkin. Finn and Gratton fired at once – and two hairy bodies fell across the threshold of the door, fur smouldering.

As the other Bloodkin drew back, with howls of rage and fright, Gratton and Finn turned and ran.

Several times more they repeated the process – lurking by the doorway of a chamber or corridor, waiting for the Bloodkin to try to enter at the other end. Not all of their shots found targets – and sometimes they were the targets, for there were Slavers too among the horde of pursuers, with their own heatlances. But the aliens kept themselves well hidden behind the bulky shapes of the Bloodkin, and were unable to aim with accuracy. Finn and Gratton continued their slow retreat unscathed.

And finally they reached their destination. The crowd of people was standing in an empty corridor, clustered nervously together, looking as if they could not work out what to do next. There was no sign of Baer – but Finn was sure that the door halfway along the corridor led to the food storeroom that he had been seeking.

As if in confirmation, one of the women gestured to the door. "He's in there," she said shakily.

Finn looked exasperated. Of course, the humans were too nervous of Baer to follow him into the narrow confines of the storeroom. But before Finn or Gratton could speak, the iris-door opened, revealing the huge shape of Baer, grinning savagely.

"I found your mousehole," he rumbled. "Now can you get it through to these folks whose side I'm on?"

"You go on into the vault," Finn said – and, despite everything, found himself half-smiling.

Baer snorted and turned away, and as he vanished through the hole that Finn had cut in the wall the crowd of people – urged on by Finn and Gratton – reluctantly followed. Finn and Gratton went through last, but not before turning and firing a warning blast at a Bloodkin who had risked opening the door at the end of the corridor.

In a moment all of them were in the vault, where the people were either staring watchfully at Baer or else peering nervously around at the shadowed metal walls and the stacks of huge, strange cases.

Finn glanced past Baer, and saw that Josh was lying half-propped against one of the cases. His eyes were still closed, but he seemed to be breathing normally.

"He woke up once," Baer rumbled, "took a look at me, an' fainted again. He'll be okay."

Finn nodded gratefully, and got back to business. "Gratton, take your people out through the tunnel. Use your heatlance to make an opening in the metal cover – and when you're out, get down the slope and into the woods. Then head south. Baer and I'll find you."

"Hope so, young fella," Gratton said cheerfully. "Us folks've got a lotta thanks t' say."

"It's not over yet," Finn reminded him. "Slavers could be waiting for you out there."

"Prob'ly not," Baer put in surprisingly. "They likely figure we're trapped in here – an' they'll be comin' after us any time now."

Finn saw that he could be right. The unimaginative aliens would not necessarily have worked out that the humans might have a way out of the tunnel. When the attack came, it would come through the storeroom – for a while, anyway. Perhaps for just long enough.

"We'll make them think we *are* trapped," Finn decided, "if we put up a fight from here. Baer, can you take Josh out with the others?"

"Nope," Baer said firmly. "If you're gonna stay an' fight, I'm stayin' too. These folks can take your pa."

"We'll see to him, Finn," Gratton said quickly. At once two men hoisted Josh to his feet and hurried towards the tunnel, half-dragging him. As rapidly, the others crowded out of the vault, vanishing into the tunnel's depths.

Before Finn or Baer could move, the sizzling crimson ray of a heatlance blasted in through the hole in the vault wall, passing harmlessly between them.

"War's startin' up again," Baer remarked.

Finn slid towards the edge of the gap, thrust his own lance into it and fired. There was a howl of agony, and a returning barrage of blazing rays that filled the gap with crimson light. Then there was silence – and Finn, warily peering past the edge of the gap, saw that the attackers had temporarily retreated from the storeroom, leaving a dead Bloodkin behind.

"Speakin' of wars," Baer went on calmly, as if nothing had happened, "here's somethin' of yours."

He reached to his belt and drew out a knife – Finn's

hunting knife. "Found it stickin' in some fella back there."

Finn took it gratefully, but then his attention was dragged back to the gap. The storeroom door had opened again, and a group of Bloodkin were edging nervously in, driven by three Slavers who kept well to the rear. Another raking blast of Finn's lance felled two of the Bloodkin, and again the group fled back to safety.

In the new lull, Finn saw that Baer was roaming the vault, inspecting the stacked cases. And Finn also then noticed, for the first time, how much brighter the vault was. It was now the light of the sun, not the moon, that was streaming in from the far end of the tunnel.

"Interestin' stuff," Baer was muttering. "Wonder what's in these things, worth stickin' away in a place like this?"

"I wish it was weapons," Finn replied. "I don't know how long this lance will last."

"Then maybe it's time we got goin'," Baer said. "Step back a bit."

Finn drew back, puzzled, then understanding as Baer, with an effortless surge of strength, heaved one of the huge cases over towards the hole in the wall. As effortlessly, he then hoisted another on top of it, to make a weighty barricade of metal.

"That won't hold 'em long," he rumbled, "but it'll make 'em think we're still here."

Together, he and Finn moved quickly into the tunnel. Ahead they saw a blaze of brightness. Gratton had cut a sizeable wedge of metal out of the covering at the tunnel mouth – large enough even for Baer.

"Real thoughtful fella," Baer grinned, moving forward.

But some instinct made Finn pause, and glance back. He was just in time to see powerful Bloodkin hands thrusting aside the two heavy cases. And through the opening poured a roaring mob of at least fifteen Bloodkin.

They saw at once that the vault was empty. They also saw the lone figure of Finn, crouching in the entrance to the tunnel. As more Bloodkin surged in, followed by the spindly forms of half a dozen Slavers, the savage roaring reached a terrifying crescendo.

At once the air turned scarlet with the hissing flashes of heatlances, flaring and blazing around Finn as he flattened himself back against the tunnel wall. But as the mass of Bloodkin charged across the vault, the turmoil made the Slavers' aim unsure, and none of the rays found its target.

But Finn's did. The blast from his lance scythed across the faces of the Bloodkin in the lead, briefly halting the charge as the others stumbled over the crumpling bodies. Again and again Finn fired, desperately, knowing that he did not dare to turn and run, now, and expose his back to the Slavers' fire.

But as he kept firing, one of his shots found a different target. It struck the largest of the metal cases that Baer had flung across the gap – melting through the case, blazing in among the contents.

Finn was never to know precisely what had been stored in the vault, in those cases marked USAF. But there was no doubt his wish – that they held some kind of weapon – was answered.

The half-melted case erupted in a volcanic blast of light and fire.

The shock of the explosion hurled Finn backwards, deeper into the tunnel, and flung the Bloodkin and Slavers in tangled heaps across the floor of the vault.

And then they vanished, into crushing blackness.

The force of the explosion finished the job that time had begun on the weakened metal of the vault. In a thunderous, bellowing cascade, the entire vault collapsed inward, burying Bloodkin and Slavers alike under tons of earth and ruptured metal.

15

Another Monster

ON EITHER SIDE of a small forest clearing, two songbirds were exchanging bursts of end-of-the-day melody, untroubled by the fine drizzle that was falling, or by the oddly assorted collection of people gathered under the trees.

Under a tall evergreen, on one side of the clearing, the surviving humans from the Slaver base sat round the remains of a fire. They were even more ragged than they had been while in captivity, and many of them wore makeshift, bloodstained bandages. Yet there was a brightness in their eyes that had not been there some days before, and a liveliness in their voices as they murmured among themselves. Even if now and then one of them might fall silent and stare into nothingness, and shiver – but not because of the light summer rain.

Beneath another tree, across the clearing, Gratton sat with old Josh. Josh's back and chest were swathed in ragged bandages, but it was clear that he was healing. Both men seemed animated, enjoying their talk and the open air, and the freedom.

But nearby, pacing back and forth on his own, Baer was not enjoying himself. He might have joined Josh and Gratton, for they at least had grown used to him, even if the others were still unnerved by his presence. But Baer was in no mood for idle chat.

He was deeply troubled about Finn. He knew that Finn
had never wholly recovered from the shock of what he had
seen, and learned, in the Slaver base. And, now that they
were safe and could relax a little, that knowledge had been
preying heavily on Finn's mind. The life had gone out of
him; he had become withdrawn, silent, morose, wrapped
in an inner shadow that grew darker with every day.

Baer knew that it was up to him to try to free Finn from
the shadow, for only he fully understood why it was there.
But so far there had been no chance to do so, ever since
they had emerged from the tunnel leading out of the
collapsed vault . . .

It was early morning, bright with sunlight, for the entire
battle and flight from the base had taken a surprisingly
short time. The grassy slope was empty as Finn and Baer
raced down it, proving that Baer had been right. The
aliens had thought they were trapped in the vault, had not
been able to anticipate that they might escape through the
tunnel.

But Baer knew it would be only a short breathing space.
There were still Slavers alive in the base – and they would
be mustering their forces, readying whirlsleds for a
vengeful pursuit.

As they plunged into the woods at the foot of the slope,
Finn also knew that they were not yet safe. But in a way
he was glad of the fact. The need to stay alert, keep
moving, perhaps to stand and fight again, would keep him
from thinking. And he was not yet ready to think about
what he had seen, and what he had realized, in the Slaver
laboratory. If he would ever be ready.

Meanwhile he was busy following the trail southwards
left by the fleeing humans. And in less than a kilometre he

and Baer had overtaken them. The people were sprawled on the soft turf, looking limply exhausted, some of them weeping from combined fatigue and fear: Many were dangerously weakened by the wounds they had suffered in the fighting. And of course all of the women were, one way or another, carrying children.

Only Gratton had the strength to rise, to greet Finn with delight, while eyeing Baer warily.

"These folks're finished," Gratton said. "Can't run no more. It'd kill 'em – an' y'r pa too."

"All right," Finn said calmly. He glanced over to where Josh was lying, still more than half unconscious. "You can stay here and patch them up as best you can. When you've rested, keep moving south. I'll go back and try to draw the Slavers off."

"An' him?" Gratton asked, glancing at Baer.

Finn's eyes flashed. "I told you before, he's my friend. I wouldn't be here if it wasn't for him – and nor would most of you people."

As Gratton nodded, looking chastened, a weak but determined voice spoke from the huddle of people. "If that's so, then I got a debt owed t' him more'n anybody."

It was Josh, who had wakened at the sound of Finn's voice and was struggling to lift himself to a sitting position. Finn went to him swiftly. "Never mind debts," he said. "Rest yourself. Baer will look after you."

Baer, who had been glowering at Gratton, looked unhappy at that. "I better come with you, Finn," he said. "You're hurtin' too."

Finn glanced down at the wound across his ribs. Though it still hurt, he had almost forgotten about it – and certainly most of the bleeding had stopped. "I'm all right. And . . . I need to be alone a while." His mouth twisted, the shadow of his inner torment showing clearly in his eyes. "I'll be back."

Then he turned towards the forest and was gone.

Shortly Finn was standing once again among the evergreens at the foot of the slope that led up to the Slaver
base. And curving down the gentle grassy incline, he saw
what he had expected. Two whirlsleds, moving at speed,
with four spywings aloft in the clear sky. The deadly
machines, Finn knew, would be able to overtake the
humans within a few minutes and then no one would
survive.

Calmly, he stepped out into view.

Then he pretended to start, as if just seeing the whirlsleds. He turned, running back into the forest, but halt-
ingly as if he were carrying an injury. And he moved on
an angle towards the west, well away from the trail made
by the escapers.

A glance behind showed the whirlsleds altering course
in his direction, the spywings following suit.

For hours, Finn led the aliens and their creatures on a
wild chase. The shadow of inner horror was pushed to the
back of his mind as he concentrated on his tactics. Time
and again he would seem accidentally to show himself,
among the trees, and the aliens and their batwinged
watchers would race forward on the attack. Then Finn
would melt back into the forest, leaving them to sweep
back and forth, searching – until it was time to give them
another tantalizing glimpse.

In those hours he led his pursuers far to the west, into a
richly tangled and marshy region of wilderness. There he
left them, busy with their mechanical search patterns,
while he slipped away invisibly towards the south.

Meanwhile Gratton and the others, urged on by Baer's
glowering impatience, had bandaged the more serious
wounds – using healing herbs gathered under Josh's

126

expert direction – and had found the strength to struggle on.

Baer provided a powerful arm to support Josh, and they were soon deep in talk. Neither pain nor weakness could keep Josh from wanting to know everything that had happened to his foster son since the Slavers had come to the village. And Baer, for his part, wanted to talk to someone about the dire effect on Finn of what he had seen in the Slaver laboratory.

Most of all, he wanted to talk to Finn. But when Finn rejoined them, at the end of the day, with the assurance that they were now safe, it was not a time for talking. Weariness had overtaken Finn, so that he could barely stay awake long enough for Baer to tend his wound.

And in the days that followed, as the small group struggled on, there was also no time to talk. Finn spent the days restlessly wandering into the wilds – scouting ahead, hunting to feed the group. And at night he was silent, aloof, wrapped in his own dark thoughts. The others, enjoying their freedom and absorbed in the weary task of travelling, hardly noticed. But Josh was worried, and Baer fretted visibly.

So, on that rain-dampened evening in the forest clearing, Baer was pacing and fretting, waiting for Finn to return. And when Gratton left Josh to amble over to the others, Baer moved across to join the old man. Josh's tough old body had regained much of its strength, but his eyes were as troubled as Baer's.

"You gonna try talkin' t' him t'day?" Josh asked.

"If I hafta sit on him," Baer growled. "He's eatin' at himself inside – won't be anythin' left, soon enough."

"Them dam' marks . . ." Josh began.

"Not the marks. Marks're just identification – Slavers put 'em on any kid born in a base." Baer glanced down at the pattern of dots on his own arm, less visible now that the singed hair was regrowing. "It's what they mean that's killin' Finn. He can't live with the idea that he's . . ."

"Another of the monsters that the Slavers make," said a flat voice behind them.

Baer turned. Finn was standing gazing at them dully, his eyes dark with pain and horror, as if he were seeing some terrible vision invisible to the others.

"Yep," Baer said in an equally flat voice. "Just one of us monsters."

Finn sat down abruptly, his face twisting. "I mean no offence, Baer. You are what you are. But I . . . I thought I was human . . ."

He fell silent, staring into space. And as Josh looked at Baer hopefully, Baer scratched his beard, gathered his thoughts, and took a deep breath.

"Finn," he began, "we been travellin' together a while now, an' I figure there's some trust grown between us. Now I wanta talk awhile, an' you're gonna listen. An' you gotta see that what I say is true, an' *feel* it in your gut − so's you can live with yourself."

He paused, encouraged to see that Finn had turned his agonized gaze on him.

"Now, truth is," Baer continued, "you got yourself born from some poor girl in a Slaver centre. Some Slaver messed around in his laboratory, an' outa that you got born the way you are." Baer's voice deepened into a scornful rumble. "But if you stop with just that truth, boy, you're a bigger dam' fool than I think."

Finn blinked, and frowned, but Baer went on.

"Whatever that Slaver did, Finn, he did to bits of *humans*. Your real pa an' ma, they hadta be just as human as Josh here. An' that makes you human, too. As anybody can see, lookin' at you. Only two things make you different from any other young fella. One is, you got some funny marks on your arm. *Two* is, you got a kinda natural

128

gift for the wilderness that'd make you think you'd been raised by wolves, not people."

"That's sure 'nough true," Josh put in. "Ain't never been his like, in the wilds."

"I know it," Baer said. "That's how come you stayed alive, Finn, 'fore Josh found you. A natural gift. An' here's the *big* truth, boy. Just the same as Slavers gave you the marks on your arm, *Slavers gave you the other thing too!*"

Finn jumped as if he had been stabbed, his eyes widening. But Baer hurried on.

"It's gotta be true. See, far's I ever heard, normal human kids born to slave women always die. Only the young Bloodkin live. So I reckon you're a rare one — maybe the *only one* — who's been born normal an' stayed alive. That's what was gettin' that Slaver so excited, the one that shot you. When he saw your marks, he *knew* you were special!"

"But . . ." Finn began.

"Hang on, I'm still talkin'," Baer said. "What I'm gettin' to is that I know what the Slavers are tryin' to do in those laboratories."

He paused for a moment, looking for the right words. "When we first met an' got talkin', I told you that Slavers were tryin' to breed a new kind of human. I didn't say *what* kind, 'cause I'd seen your marks, an' I didn't know how much you knew 'bout yourself. But it's like this. Slavers've got no use for humans with *minds*. Those minds get thinkin', an' inventin', an' maybe findin' ways to fight back. Slavers want people to be quiet an' do what they're told, like a buncha sheep or some other domestic critturs."

Behind Finn's puzzled frown, a glimmer of understanding was trying to break through.

"See?" Baer said. "Slavers are tryin' to breed the minds

outa people. They're tryin' to turn humans back into *animals!*"

"The Bloodkin . . ." Josh said, then flushed.

"Sure," Baer said with his lopsided grin. "Most times, they get the Bloodkin, who're dam' near animals – though not all of 'em, if I say so myself. But Bloodkin aren't good for much but fightin'. I figure the Slavers're really tryin' to make humans into animals without changin' the way they look."

Baer's bass chuckle rumbled. "Seems, though, they don't have much luck. Most times, the normal kids die. An' when one does live, he gets away – how, we'll prob'ly never know. An' even then, that one turns out to have a real good mind – an' only *one thing* about him that's any way like an animal. He's got a knowledge an' instinct for the wilderness as good as any wild crittur – born deep inside him, in his blood an' bones."

As Finn sat silent, lost in a tangle of thoughts and emotions, Baer reached over and prodded the dots on his arm with a thick finger. "You oughta be proud of these marks," he rumbled. "They mean you're special. You shoulda been one of the Slavers' successes – but you turned out to be their biggest failure." The crooked grin flashed. "An' so am I. They made me a Bloodkin, but I got born with a bit more humanity in me. An' 'cause of that, I'm just about the worst thing that coulda happened – to Slavers."

He gripped Finn's shoulder and shook him lightly. "Only now I figure maybe it's *you* that's the worst thing, for them. You're all human, mind an' body, heart an' soul – but mixed up in there is a crittur that belongs to the wilds. An', Finn, mosta this big dam' country is wilderness. Out here there's nobody – no Slaver for sure – who can even *find* you, if you don't wanta be found. An' now . . . the Slavers've gone an' got you mad at 'em."

130

Baer's grin took on an edge of savagery. "When they made you an' me, Finn Ferral, it was like they made knives to cut their throats with."

16

The Pursuit Continues

FOR A LONG time, as the night drew in, the talk went on. And afterwards, while all the others slept, Finn remained wakeful, his mind churning.

Baer's words and their truths had impressed him deeply. Though the shadows of horror remained in his mind, and might remain a long time, Finn sensed that it no longer threatened to overwhelm him.

Despite the shattering truth of his origin, Baer had made him see that nothing had truly changed. He was, in himself, the same as he had been before. He was still Finn Ferral – a human being, and a huntsman.

And when he had fully grasped the stunning simplicity of that fact, the shadow began to recede.

Then, with some shame, Finn was reminded of another fact. In the depths of his misery and horror, he had almost lost sight of the grim task that he had taken upon himself, the day he had first left the village. Old Josh was free now – but his task was only half-done. And it had been delayed too long.

By sun-up, even without sleep, Finn felt strangely refreshed, and whole – as if he had regained some part of himself that had seemed lost. Even Gratton, who knew nothing of Finn's inner torment, noticed the change when he strode purposefully over.

"Y' look like y' slept good," Gratton said.

"Something like that," Finn smiled. "What's on your mind?"

"It's the folks," Gratton said, looking a little apologetic. "We been kinda wonderin' where we're headin', what you reckon we sh'd do."

Then it was Finn's turn to look disconcerted. "I . . . I haven't been thinking much about it. Just about getting as far away from the Slavers as we can."

"Sure, us too," Gratton nodded. "Only thing is, these folks're kinda lost. They don't wanna go back t' their villages, in case Slavers come again. An' the women – people ain't gonna make 'em welcome, not with them kids."

Finn agreed, bleakly, knowing something of the narrow fearfulness of villagers.

"An' we know," Gratton went on, "that you ain't gonna stay with us forever. We reckon we gotta get somewheres where we c'n fend for ourselves, an' stay clear of Slavers."

"Where's that?" rumbled the deep voice of Baer, coming up to them. "The moon?"

"Nope," Gratton said determinedly. "See, I come from a village a long ways west, an' we usedta hear about a place even farther west. Called the Wasteland. Seems Slavers don't go there much – an' there're folks livin' there, free."

Baer snorted. "Mister, I been on the Wasteland. It's smack up against the mountains where I come from. It's all sand, desert, dry as old bones. An' there're other places that make the desert seem friendly. An' critturs like out of a bad dream. But I never saw a sign of humans there."

Old Josh had wandered over in time to hear Baer's words, and he chortled. "If there're folks there, they wouldn't likely come out an' say how-do when they saw *you* passin'."

They all laughed at that, but Gratton went on quickly. "I know it's rough country. But if people *are* livin' there, maybe we could too, an' be safe from Slavers."

"If you live at all," Baer growled.

Finn saw Gratton's jaw set stubbornly, and broke in. "Baer's right, you'd probably have a hard time of it. But you're right, too – you have to find a place for yourselves. If I was you, I'd probably go the same way."

"No chance," Gratton asked hopefully, "that y'd come along?"

Finn shook his head. "I've got to get Josh somewhere safe, and get on with something I've got to do. Could be I'll head west, but I'd want to move at my own speed."

"What's that about me?" Josh leaned forward, gripping Finn's arm. "I know y're twitchin' t' get goin' an' look for Jena. Wish I c'd come with y'. But as it is, least I c'n do is not hold y' up."

Before Finn could speak, Josh turned to Gratton. "Friend, I know a thing or two 'bout livin' off the wilds – been a huntsman all my life. Not as good as Finn, but good enough. What y' say if I come west with y'?"

A huge grin spread over Gratton's scarred face. "I'd say y'd be welcome, an' then some. Just wait'll I tell the folks that!" Nodding to Finn, he hurried away to join the others.

Finn looked at Josh. "Is that what you really want to do?"

The old man shrugged. "Son, what I really want is some magic that'll bring Jena back this minute. But there ain't none, an' I'm too old t' go an' look for her. So I'll go with these folks, an' be glad of it. And then maybe *you* c'n go, an' do what needs doin'."

"I will," Finn said, with a tightness in his throat. For a long moment the two men looked at each other in silence – with love and respect, and much anxiety and sadness.

134

Both knew that once they parted they might never see each other again. Both knew that was the way it had to be.

Beside them, Baer growled impatiently. "I hate to butt in, but either of you two wild men have the littlest idea where to start lookin' for your girl?"

Josh shook his head sadly. "All I know is, when we was separated, the sled carryin' Jena seemed t' swing west."

Finn agreed. "That's the sled we were trying to track, Baer, till we got sidetracked. And you said yourself there's a chance she was taken to the big Slaver centre in the mountains."

Baer sighed. "Sure, a chance. An' there's a chance they turned south, or swung back east, or went anywhere. It's a great big country, Finn."

But Finn had a light in his eye that had not been there for days. "I know it. But I can only go one road at a time. So I'm going west, and see what's to be seen."

"That figures," Baer grunted. "But you got one thing wrong."

"What?" Finn asked sharply.

Baer's eyes twinkled. "Son, we've stirred things up some round here. Slavers everywhere will know by now what's happened – somethin' that's never happened before, people comin' in an' rescuin' slaves. So they'll be watchin' real careful for more trouble. An' that means things could get excitin' – lotsa Slavers stickin' out their necks for ol' Baer to chop off." The deep chuckle rose in his chest. "So *you're* not goin' west, young Finn. *We* are."

And the crowd of people gathered around Gratton, across the clearing, looked over in surprise, wondering what it was that had made the big Bloodkin and the young huntsman suddenly burst out laughing.

135

Douglas Hill
**Warriors of the Wasteland 2:
Creatures of the Claw**

The Claw has gone hunting.

And what The Claw wants to catch, gets caught.

Finn Ferral is on the run, and this time there's no escape from his hunter. The Claw is the enemy of all free men – the enemy of freedom itself. And he's on Finn's tail.

Finn has entered the bleak and brutal Wasteland, and his journey looks like it's coming to an end. For The Claw is the servant of the alien Slavers – his family's captors – and they will never let Finn be free . . .

Douglas Hill
**Warriors of the Wasteland 3:
Alien Citadel**

One way or another, this is the end of the Wasteland . . .

Time is running out for Finn Ferral and his warrior allies. Close behind them is the terrifying army of the Slavers. Ahead are the treacherous Firesands. Either way, they're facing certain death – or worse.

And the last hope of freedom fades when Finn is finally captured, and dragged to the rotten core of the Slavers' world – the Alien Citadel . . .

Douglas Hill
Galactic Warlord
Book one of the Last Legionary Quartet

He stands alone . . . his planet, Moros, destroyed by unknown forces. His one vow – to wreak a terrible vengeance on the sinister enemy.

But Keill Randor, the Last Legionary, cannot conceive the evil force he will unleash in his crusade against the Warlord, the master of destruction, and his murderous army, the Deathwing.

A selected list of titles available from Macmillan and Pan Books

The prices shown below are correct at the time of going to press. However, Macmillan Publishers reserve the right to show new retail prices on covers which may differ from those previously advertised.

WARRIORS OF THE WASTELAND

1. The Huntsman	Douglas Hill	£3.99
2. Creatures of the Claw	Douglas Hill	£3.99
3. Alien Citadel	Douglas Hill	£3.99

LAST LEGIONARY QUARTET

1. Galactic Warlord	Douglas Hill	£3.99
2. Deathwing over Veynaa	Douglas Hill	£3.99
3. Day of the Starwind	Douglas Hill	£3.99
4. Planet of the Warlord	Douglas Hill	£3.99

All Macmillan titles can be ordered at your local bookshop or are available by post from:

Book Service by Post
PO Box 29, Douglas, Isle of Man IM99 1BQ

Credit cards accepted. For details:
Telephone: 01624 675137
Fax: 01624 670923
E-mail: bookshop@enterprise.net

Free postage and packing in the UK.
Overseas customers: add £1 per book (paperback)
and £3 per book (hardback).